THE CHANG

The Changing Scenes of Life

FRED SECOMBE

Fount
An Imprint of HarperCollins*Publishers*

Fount Paperbacks is an Imprint of
HarperCollins*Religious*
Part of HarperCollins*Publishers*
77-85 Fulham Palace Road, London W6 8JB

First published in Great Britain in 1997
by HarperCollins*Publishers*
This edition 1998

1 3 5 7 9 10 8 6 4 2

A catalogue record for this book
is available from the British Library.

ISBN 000 628067 6

Printed and bound in Great Britain by
Caledonian International Book Manufacturing Ltd, Glasgow

To the Right Reverend Hewlett Thompson,
Bishop of Exeter, in appreciation of his
pastoral care during my incumbency
in the London Diocese.

'Well, you know what they do say, Vicar. Make hail while the sun shines.' With these words, our newly appointed domestic help, Mrs Cooper, left the Vicarage after her interview, her face split with a grin wider than that of a Cheshire Cat. As my wife, Eleanor, and I watched her go down the drive she said, 'I never thought we would find another Mrs Richards. If her cooking and cleaning are as good as her malapropisms, we have found a treasure.' Our previous help, Mrs Jenkins, had to tender her resignation when her one and only son, who had emigrated to Australia, offered her a 'granny flat' in his newly built house and a share in the good life he had made for himself. Mrs Richards had been my landlady in my previous parish in Pontywen, an elderly widow with a heart of gold and a tongue which mutilated the English language.

It was some eight months since I had arrived in Abergelly, a large valley parish in West Monmouthshire. During that time I discovered that I had inherited a mountain of problems which had accumulated during my predecessor's incumbency of thirty years, and for which he had been awarded a canonry. In those eight months I had managed to recruit a band of volunteers who had erected a prefabricated building to serve as a church on a new housing estate, and who had given a facelift to a church hall in the doldrums of decrepitude. My wife, a general practitioner, had given up a flourishing practice in Pontywen to set up a surgery in a council house on the housing estate of Brynfelin. Our two children, David aged five and Elspeth aged three, were in the care of Marlene, a nineteen-year-old who had come with us from Pontywen.

My sole clerical assistance was provided by the Reverend Hugh Thomas, a deacon of some six months' standing, whose chief claim to fame in Abergelly was his prowess as an outside half for the local rugby team, described by the sporting press as 'the discovery of the year'. On a number of occasions he had appeared at the altar with a bruised countenance, and once with a leg injury which prevented him from kneeling. Apart from those drawbacks he was an enthusiastic colleague with considerable ability as a preacher and diligent in visiting the houses on the estate as a prelude to the dedication of the church in a week's time.

Christmas was a fortnight away. I had persuaded the Parochial Church Council to agree to the first Midnight Mass in the parish, which would be held in the new church of St David's as a means of creating interest on the estate. The unpretentious building, which was the gift of a steel magnate in Cardiff, had cost a mere £200 to erect. The furniture had been either donated by various churches, non-conformist and anglican, or bought at a ludicrously low price from builders' yards. The seating was a mixture of benches, pews and chairs which could accommodate two hundred and fifty worshippers. In the sanctuary was an altar which had survived the bombing of a church in Cardiff, and the altar rails were homemade by Jack

Richards, the fish and chip king of Abergelly who had acted as foreman of the building operations. The Mothers' Union had donated the altar cloth and the brass cross. My Curate had suggested that the church should be called St Heinz since it had such a variety of church furniture.

There was great enthusiasm amongst the volunteer workers who had created this new place of worship, but very little on the estate itself at the prospect of having their own church. Hugh Thomas had brought back tales of complete indifference. One old lady told him, 'I'm Conservative and proud of it'. The only interest shown by parents with young children was whether it would be somewhere to take them 'off the streets'. On other occasions he had seen a slight movement of the curtains while the lady of the house checked the identity of the caller who had knocked at the door. This was followed by a deafening silence from within as she waited for the clerical caller to depart from her doorstep. It said much for Hugh that such reaction to his visiting did not dampen his enthusiasm: 'If we begin with only a handful of worshippers we can build on that foundation.' His words were addressed to the committee appointed to organize the preparations for the dedication. It had been decided that the service would be followed by a tea and concert. Later in the week there would be an evening of rock and roll which was calculated to arouse the interest of young people on the estate.

I could have performed the dedication myself since the new church was a temporary building due to be replaced in ten years' time by a permanent church. However, the Bishop had offered his services as a mark of his encouragement to the clergy and congregation in their 'mission to the people on the hill', as he put it. When I told Tom Beynon, the People's Warden, what the Bishop had said he suggested that his Lordship must have been listening to 'that record on the wireless about the folk who live on the hill'. 'In any case, Vicar,' he went on, 'it's about time that Abergelly had some attention paid to it by the powers that be. We've been the underdogs for far too long. What's more, if it hadn't been for the fact that we've got a live wire in the Vicarage at last, we would still be the underdogs.'

'In all fairness to the Bishop,' I replied, 'if I am to be described as a live wire, it is he who was responsible for its installation in the Vicarage.'

After the interview with Mrs Cooper, I went to the Abergelly Secondary Modern school where Ivor Hodges, the Vicar's Warden, was headmaster. If ever anyone could be described as a right-hand man he was it. From my first Sunday in the parish when I met him in the choir vestry, he had been a tower of strength. Physically, he did not come into that category. Tall, painfully thin, pale, with hair which was rapidly receding and with a prominent Adam's apple, he was the antithesis of his fellow warden who was short, sturdy and with a face which bore blue scars, the trademarks of the mines. Ivor had stepped into the breech when his predecessor had resigned in a fit of pique. He had taken control of the belltower when the captain and his fellow ringers had walked out. In all, the debt I owed to him was immense. Now, once again I was calling on him for help. Evan Roberts, the organist at the parish church, had phoned that morning with the information that he would not be able to play the piano for the concert but that he would be available to perform at the harmonium for the dedication service. Ivor's music master was an accomplished pianist. Inevitably my thoughts turned to my warden.

As I came through the school gates I was greeted by the strains of 'The Blue Danube' sung by treble voices pouring forth from the opened windows of the hall. The music came to an abrupt end, followed by a loud admonition from the master informing the pupils that they could do much better than that. The next minute I was knocking on the door of the headmaster's office. I was told to come in and, entering the sanctum, was confronted by the sight of Ivor's balding head bent over the papers on his desk.

'Yes?' he enquired without looking up.

'Please, sir,' I replied, 'can I borrow your music master?' He sat bolt upright with a smile on his face. 'And one more question, sir,' I went on, 'why are the windows of your school hall wide open on a wintry morning?'

'Good morning, Vicar,' he said. 'In answer to your first question, yes, if he is willing to be borrowed. In answer to your second question, after every school assembly we have to open the windows to ventilate the hall since so many young bodies in rude health have filled it to capacity. Please sit down and explain yourself. Would you care for a coffee while you do so?'

He pressed a buzzer on his desk and his secretary appeared from a side door. 'Could we have two coffees, please, Mrs Williams? Mine as usual and I think the Vicar likes his with milk but no sugar.' I nodded. Mrs Williams, a matronly lady, bespectacled and neatly dressed in jumper

5

and skirt, smiled at me and then disappeared into the back room.

'The woman's a treasure,' he said. 'Very organized and energetic. She has had a tragic life. Her husband was killed in a colliery accident and her son, an only child, was killed in a road accident. The school has become an antidote for her troubled mind. That and her singing. She has a glorious contralto voice and occasionally sings the solo part in the oratorios put on in her chapel.'

'She would make a marvellous Buttercup,' I commented. He looked at me in bewilderment for a moment. 'Or even a Fairy Queen,' I added.

'Light dawns,' he replied. 'You are talking Gilbert and Sullivan. Of course, you and Dr Secombe were the leading lights in the Pontywen society. Well, if you want to start one here the school hall is at your disposal. Graham Webb would love to be its musical director. Is that why you want to borrow him?'

'Nothing as exciting,' I said. 'I wondered if he would play the piano for our concert after the dedication. I have just had a phone call from Evan Roberts to say that he can play the harmonium for the service but will have to dash away afterwards, something to do with his union.'

'You can go and ask him yourself, once you have had your coffee,' replied the headmaster. So it was that Abergelly Church Gilbert and Sullivan Society was conceived; like so many births, accidental rather than planned.

The music master had finished his session with his pupils and was sitting at the piano improvising on the theme of 'The Blue Danube' when I entered the hall. Graham Webb was a fresh-faced young man in his late twenties, untidily dressed, with the knot of his tie some distance away from the collar of his shirt, and his jacket unbuttoned. He looked up startled when I appeared alongside him.

'Hello, Vicar,' he said. 'What brings you here?'

'You do,' I replied.

He raised his eyebrows. 'I am flattered. What can I do for you?'

'I wonder if you could do me a great favour. The church organist is unable to provide the accompaniment at the piano for a concert we are holding to celebrate the opening of a new church we have erected in the Brynfelin estate. Would you possibly fill the breech?'

'When is it?' he asked.

'Next Tuesday week,' I replied. 'I know it's short notice but I should be more than grateful if you could oblige.'

'I'm sure I can manage that,' he said. 'Are you and your good lady going to sing some Gilbert and Sullivan? I understand from Aneurin Williams that you two are devoted to the Savoy operas.' Aneurin Williams was the music master at Pontywen Grammar School and the musical director of the Gilbert and Sullivan Society I had founded there.

'We had thought of it but decided against it, since Evan Roberts, our organist, is not exactly a talented accompanist. Now that you are to be at the piano, I am sure that my wife will be only too pleased to sing, not to mention myself, of course.'

'It so happens that I too am a Gilbert and Sullivan devotee,' he said. 'Have you considered forming a society here in Abergelly? If you have, then you have a musical director at your service.' He continued, 'I am sure I can

7

persuade the Head to give permission for the use of the hall for rehearsals.'

'You don't have to do that,' I replied. 'He has just told me that permission is granted.'

When I went back to the Vicarage at lunchtime, Eleanor was in the kitchen frying bacon and eggs for our midday meal. 'I'll be glad when Mrs Cooper takes over this job,' she said, addressing the bacon and eggs. 'It's enough to do running a surgery without having to run a kitchen.'

'In that case,' I replied, 'you will not approve of me doing two jobs.'

She turned from the frying pan and stared at me. 'What on earth do you mean?' she enquired.

'I have just more of less agreed with a young man that I shall start another G & S Society in Abergelly,' I replied. There was a silence as we continued to look at each other.

'You mean that the music master from Ivor's school has talked you into another commitment when you are surrounded by a mountain of them,' she said quietly. 'Some mothers do have them, and your mother certainly had one when she had you. You can't cope with what you have to do because of your duties as Vicar without taking something on which is totally unnecessary, just a piece of selfish indulgence on your part.'

'My dear love,' I replied, 'it is only a few months ago that you told me that the stomach trouble I had was due to stress and nothing more. What is better to cure stress than to do something I enjoy and so do you, if it comes to that. In any case, as you know, the first six months of rehearsals would be confined to music once a week and not involve me in production work at all.'

8

'That is called special pleading, Frederick, as you well know.' The tone of her voice had lost its cutting edge.

'By the way,' I added, 'he said that he would be delighted to provide the accompaniment if we wanted to sing some G & S at the concert.'

'That I wouldn't mind,' she said, 'but I certainly think you should consider carefully before deciding to form a new society in Abergelly.'

'That sounds better,' I answered, and kissed her.

'Blandishments will get you nowhere! If you have no objection, will you let me get on with our lunch.' She went back to her frying pan. 'Now look what you have done,' she said reproachfully. 'It has been cremated rather than cooked.'

That afternoon I drove out to Llandyfrig to collect a bundle of redundant hymn-books and prayer-books from the Rural Dean, the Reverend Llewellyn Evans. He was a native of Carmarthenshire, a son of the farm whose first language was Welsh until he was ordained in a diocese where English was the norm in almost all the parishes. As a result he had spent the next thirty years cultivating a pseudo-Oxbridge accent and creating a unique vocabulary which bore no relation to that which is found in any English dictionary. Most of his words were the result of adding 'ness' to nouns, adjectives or adverbs, and so beauty became 'beautifulness'. He would preach about the 'wonderfulness' of Creation. Moreover, as someone born of Welsh farming stock he was more inclined to give in kind rather than money. Thus it was that he offered to supply the new place of worship on the Brynfelin estate with the left-overs from his church as the result of a donation of new books by the local Squire, who had grown tired of using the dog-eared editions which had been in use since the turn of the century. As someone who had no means of paying for anything in the new 'prefab', I felt I had to gather any crumbs which fell from the rich man's table.

Llandyfrig was a parish which had escaped the rape of the valley by the colliery owners. It was a green oasis in an industrial desert. There the Rural Dean lived in splendour, his Vicarage drive ornamented by flower borders and flanked by two rolling lawns in immaculate condition. The house was a stone-built Victorian mansion containing twenty-two rooms, most of which were furnished with bargains acquired at various auctions down through the years. It looked out on to farmland across the valley, a scene which would have been replicated in every parish before the Industrial Revolution. After I had parked my car outside the front of the Vicarage, I stood for a few minutes enjoying the peace and the scenery.

My musings were ended by an assault upon my person by a cocker spaniel which had appeared from nowhere. Then the bulky figure of the Rural Dean emerged through the front door. 'Mrs Evans said she thought she heard the sound of a motor car.' He always referred to his wife as 'Mrs Evans'. 'Down! Sian,' he shouted at the dog, which was leaping in front of me like a demented dervish. At his word of command, the golden-haired animal slunk through the open door of the Vicarage, where it was greeted by a torrent of Welsh from 'Mrs Evans'.

'Come on in, Vicar,' the Rural Dean said. 'I had only just come from the church with the er – donation, shall I say, to your pioneeringness in Brynfelin.' He led me into his study, where Mrs Evans had been busy with her tin of polish, its aroma filling the room. 'Sit down, please,' he invited, beckoning me into a leather armchair which seemed to have received more than its fair share of attention from his wife's labours. I sneezed violently. As I blew my nose he remarked, 'They say there's a lot of this flu business about, I hope you haven't caught any of that. You will need to be up on your toes, as they say, to be able to face the challengingness of your parish.'

'Not to worry, Mr Rural Dean,' I replied. 'I get these sneezes occasionally. It is not an attack of influenza, I can assure you. If you don't mind, I shall have to pick up your donation, as you put it, and get back to Abergelly as soon as possible. There are a hundred and one things I have to see to before the dedication, as you can imagine.'

At this stage in the conversation, Mrs Evans came into the study. She was a tiny, thin lady, whose greying hair straggled around her emaciated features, crying out for attention from a hairbrush. 'Would you like a cup of tea, Vicar?' she enquired.

'No thank you, Mrs Evans. I have just been saying that I have to get back to my parish as quickly as possible.'

She seemed relieved. 'Llewellyn,' she said, 'I have put those red hymn-books and prayer-books in my shopping bag. We'll be coming to Abergelly tomorrow to do our shopping. So we'll call at your Vicarage, Mr Secombe, to pick it up before we start.'

'With pleasure,' I replied.

I stood up. The Rural Dean seemed disappointed at the brevity of my visit. 'I'm sorry you can't stay longer,' he said, 'but there you are, the time and the tide don't stay around for ever, as that old proverb tells us.'

At that moment his wife came into the room struggling to hold her shopping bag with its burden of Llandyfrig's help for the Brynfelin estate. I jumped up. 'Please let me take that from you, Mrs Evans,' I said, 'it must be very heavy.'

She smiled as I took it from her. 'Once upon a time,' she commented, 'when I was a farmer's daughter I could have carried that on one finger. There you are, one day you will be old like us. Until then, my dear, you enjoy the strength that God gives you.' It was my first real encounter with Mrs Evans, and from that time on I regarded her as someone to respect as an ideal wife for any parsonage.

When I emptied the contents of the Rural Dean's 'donation' to Brynfelin, I looked at my desk in dismay. It was covered in a *mélange* of detached covers, stray pages and much-thumbed contents in imminent danger of parting company with their binding. The first aid required would tax the patience of Job at his best. With no more than a week or so available for the dedication service, I would have to borrow books from the parish church and then go scrounging elsewhere. As I stood surveying the liturgical debris, my wife returned from her rounds and came into the study. She joined me at the desk.

'Good heavens!' she exclaimed. 'Is this the contribution from the Rural Dean? There's only one place for this and that's the dustbin. How dare he dump such rubbish on you as his contribution to the new church, the mean old bugger.'

'Eleanor,' I said, 'control yourself. Don't forget you are in the Vicarage and you are the Vicar's wife.'

'Am I?' she replied. 'I tell you what, I would say the same thing if I was in St Paul's Cathedral. He really is meanness personified. You deserve better than that. I'll phone my father tonight to ask him if he would like to make a gift of some hymn-books and prayer-books for St David's. After all, his Christian name is David. So you could say he has an obligation to help his namesake.'

My father-in-law was a doctor in a market town on the other side of the valley. An ex-miner, he had made his way up the ladder and enjoyed the fruits of his living in a lucrative medical practice in the 'posh' part of the county.

That night I went to see how the voluntary workers were coping with the finishing touches to the building at Brynfelin. As soon as I opened the door my nostrils were invaded by the smell of fresh paint. It was being applied to the window frames by Arnold Templeman, a stocky, grey-haired bandy-legged retired painter and decorator who was barely five foot tall. He was wearing a pair of overalls which completely enveloped his lower limbs and gave the impression that his feet were directly connected to his torso. Blinking at me through his horn-rimmed spectacles he said, 'Would you mind telling Dai Elbow to put a sock in it? He's been bellowing like a foghorn in your vestry.'

David Rees, known to all in Abergelly as Dai Elbow, was engaged in completing the wiring in the small cubicle described by Arnold as 'my vestry'. His nickname was derived from the constant use of his elbow to flatten his opponents in his career as lock forward for the local rugby team. It was a career cut short by a permanent ban when his fifteenth victim was laid low and spent six weeks in hospital. Off the field he was the most congenial of men and was one of my mainstays in the work at Brynfelin. Arnold was one of the least congenial of men and was known to his fellow workers as 'the old moaner'. No sooner had the little man registered his complaint than a loud discordant rendering of Bing Crosby's 'White Christmas' burst forth. 'See what I mean,' said Arnold. 'How can I concentrate with all that noise?'

The solo was cut short when I came into the 'vestry'. 'Hello, Vic!' proclaimed Dai. 'Nearly finished the wiring for the power socket.' Whenever he spoke his conversation could be heard some distance away, and for those who were in immediate contact it was a severe attack on the eardrums.

'Well done, Dai,' I replied in a deliberately lowered tone. 'By the way, would you mind not singing? Arnold says it is interfering with his painting. You know what he's like.'

' 'E doesn't know a good voice when he 'ears one, the unsociable bugger.' This was spoken in tones which could have been heard in the street, let alone the building. 'Anyway, Vic, it looks as if everything will be finished in plenty of time for the opening,' he continued. 'What do you think of your Curate's game last Saturday? 'E going places 'e is, I can tell you.'

As he spoke the door at the back of the church opened and a voice greeted Arnold. 'How is it going, Mr Templeman?' ('Talk of the devil,' commented Dai, ''ere 'e is.')

'A lot better if Dai would stop bawling,' came the reply.

'Is the Vicar here?' Hugh Thomas asked.

'He's in the vestry with Dai. Thank God he has shut him up, I say.'

The Curate burst in upon us. Short, sturdy, dark haired, almost swarthy in countenance, his excess of energy impelled him into energetic entrances. 'Anything I can do, Vicar?' he asked. 'By the way, Dai, you're in trouble with Mr Templeman.'

'You're telling me,' replied the offender. 'It's just that he doesn't know good music when 'e 'ears it.'

'There's nothing here for you, Hugh,' I said, 'but you can come down with me to the other church hall. Jack Richards has arranged with Bevan the coal merchant to borrow his lorry to pick up the piano at eight o'clock, ready for the concert. You will be more of a help than me to load it on the wagon, that's if you are not too exhausted after your training session at the ground.'

'Vicar!' he exclaimed. 'Do I look tired? Why not come down in my car, then you can go back in yours once we have transported that old Joanna.'

Outside his ancient open-top MG was waiting. He vaulted over the closed door of the machine into the driving seat. 'You'll do yourself an injury one of these days,' I said.

'According to you, reverend sir, I am always doing myself injuries,' he replied, 'or to put it differently, others are doing me injuries.'

'Don't be cheeky, Hugh,' I told him, 'just drive off, will you please?' He put his foot on the accelerator and we shot away as if propelled by a rocket. I was more than happy to arrive at the church hall unscathed.

Jack Richards met us outside the door. From inside the hall there was a volume of noise which a dozen Dai Elbows could not create. 'It's about time that Willie James kept those kids under control,' he complained. 'I always thought that scouts should be there to help people, like taking old ladies across the road and that kind of thing. God help any old dear who would have to rely on one of that lot!'

'Don't shoot the pianist Jack,' I said, 'he's doing his best. So far he has avoided any damage to the hall now that it has been renovated.'

When we went inside, the boys were engaged in team races, and standing at the foot of the stage was the scoutmaster, a diminutive figure whose 'short' trousers belied that description by covering his kneecaps and meeting the tops of his stockings. He blinked at us through his jam-jar spectacles and moved forward to greet us, only to be bowled over by a burly adolescent intent on winning the race. When he had picked himself up and retrieved his glasses, he blew hard on his whistle. By this time the encouraging shouts had given way to raucous laughter at the sight of the collision.

'To what do we owe this honour, Vicar?' he enquired in the ludicrously deep baritone voice which emerged from his puny figure.

'We are going to take the piano to the new church ready for the concert at its opening. So if you can occupy your scouts with less physical activities for the next half hour or so, I should be more than grateful.'

'Now then, lads,' he commanded. 'Everybody into the classroom and off the floor of the hall for the time being.' There was a stampeded exit as Willie looked on helplessly. 'One at a time lads,' he shouted as bodies were squashed in competition in the doorway.

'We could do with some of them in our forwards,' commented Hugh Thomas. The scoutmaster blew his whistle but to no effect. 'Just like our forwards,' added the Curate. By the time the troops had been closeted in the classroom, Bevan the Coal made his appearance in the hall, his eyes mascaraed with coal dust. 'Right,' he said, 'where's this piano then?'

If anything merited the description 'old Joanna' it was the instrument in the church hall. Decorated with candle holders on either side, it appeared to have been made before the invention of electricity. ''Ave it got casters?' enquired the coal merchant.

'It has,' I replied, 'but they are on their way out, I am afraid.'

'Don't be afraid,' interjected my Curate, 'that's where they are going anyway.' I was about to put him in his place, but remembering that the coal merchant was present contented myself with what I thought was an admonitory stare.

'Right,' said Mr Bevan once again. Evidently it was one of his favourite words. 'Let's have it out on the pavement, then we'll put it on its side and lift it on to the lorry.'

The piano squeaked its way out of the hall until it came to repose at the back of the lorry. 'Right,' repeated the lorry owner. 'I'll put the tailboard down. Then if the Vicar and the Curate will stay at the back, Jack and me will lift the piano up at the front on to the lorry, then you two can lift up your end and shove it forward, right?' The piano was tilted on to its side. 'Right, Jack,' ordered the transporter. Up it went at the front and rested on the back of the lorry. 'Now then, Vicar, you two lift it up, while we guide it on to the lorry. Right,' he shouted. Hugh Thomas and I lifted our end and pushed. There was a cry of pain, 'Bloody 'ell,' exclaimed Mr Bevan. 'You jammed my 'and at the side by 'ere.'

Seconds later the instrument was safely aboard. At least it seemed to be safely aboard. 'Hugh and I will go up to the church and wait for you there,' I said. The Curate performed his circus act of leaping into his seat and we roared away to Brynfelin.

Half an hour later we were still waiting for the lorry to arrive. Dai Elbow had finished his wiring but stayed on to see if he could be of any assistance. Arnold Templeman had finished his labours and had gone home, leaving signs of 'wet paint' in bold letters on pieces of cardboard strewn around the hall. It was an unnecessary precaution since the smell of his labours was a sufficient indication.

After another quarter of an hour, the Curate said, 'Shall I slip down to see what has happened?' Before he could slip down, the door opened and a very embarrassed pair appeared. It was Jack Richards who was the spokesman. 'Sorry, Vicar,' he murmured, 'but when we were halfway up that steep bit of the hill by Evans' farm with that nasty bend, the piano slid down and broke the tail board and ended up in a field. It was pitch black, as you know, but we made our way to the farmhouse where the lights were all on, fortunately. Old man Evans brought a torch with him and we found the piano broken up with a dead sheep alongside it. He said he wants compensation.'

2

When I returned to the Vicarage with the news that the church hall piano had played its last notes in a field belonging to Evans the Farm, my wife was highly amused. 'I can see the headline in tomorrow's paper: "Sheep much struck by church music",' she giggled. 'What a wonderful way for that worn-out instrument to depart this life. I was about to ring my father with a request that he would donate a set of hymn-books and prayer-books for St David's. We can get the service for the opening duplicated on the parish machine. Instead I shall ask *mon père* for a new piano. Can't you see, Fred? It is providential. We could never have had music rehearsals for a G & S production, using that old scrap heap. Thank God for Bevan the Coal and his wonky tailboard, I say.'

'Earlier today,' I replied, 'you were warning me about contemplating starting a Gilbert and Sullivan Society in Abergelly. Now you are speaking about such a venture as if it were a *fait accompli*.'

'It's just another example of a light on the road to Damascus,' she said. 'The scales have been lifted from my eyes. I can see that a dose of the Savoy operas will be a vital element in the resurgence of parish life in Abergelly.'

'You are as much addicted to mixed metaphors as my Curate,' I commented, 'but I fully agree with your sentiments. So pick up that phone, sweetheart, and get cracking.'

'Fred,' she breathed, 'you can be so masterful.'

She left the sitting-room and went into the study to phone her father, singing, 'The flowers that bloom in the spring, tra la, give promise of merry sunshine'. A few minutes later she emerged and came to me as I was on my way to the kitchen to find some biscuits to accompany our nightcaps. She held me in a rib-cracking embrace and then kissed me. 'Frederick,' she announced, 'the parish has got itself a real piano at last.'

The next morning I had a phone call from Daniel Evans, Blaenymaes Farm. I had never met him but from what I could gather, he was an irascible old man. This became evident in his first words to me: 'Couldn't you have found something better than Bevan's old coal lorry to take your piano up to Brynfelin?' Before I could answer he carried on with his tirade. 'Trying to get something on the cheap. You see what happens. You've lost your piano and what's more killed one of my sheep. Now then, I want compensation for that sheep, pick of the flock she was. So that will be ten pounds and I want it straightaway. I've got to replace that sheep.' Despite his age he must have had a healthy pair of lungs. He had never stopped to breathe.

'Well, Mr Evans,' I replied, 'I am very sorry about your sheep. Evidently she must have been too slow to get out of the way when the piano came into your field. I would have thought that she would have been the first to get away if she was the pick of your flock.'

He began to bluster. 'Are you saying that I am trying to get money out of the church by false pretences? Let me tell you. It could be a lot more money I could ask for. What

20

about the damage to the hedge? Then who's going to clear up all the mess of wires and wood? I don't want my sheep injured by getting caught in those wires and things. So the sooner that rubbish is gone the better. Either I arrange for it to be carted away at once or you do something about it. Either way, it's got to go now and not tomorrow.'

By now my head was in a whirl after this machine-gun-like verbal attack. 'I will get in touch with you later today, Mr Evans,' I said, and put the phone down immediately, to avoid another battering of my eardrums.

I sat down at my desk, wondering what to do next. It was ten o'clock and I had arranged to collect some has-socks for the new church from the Reverend William Evans, Vicar of Llanybedw, known to Eleanor and me as 'Uncle Will' from his self-description on my first meeting with him. Members of his Mothers' Union had presented his church with kneelers, which they had embroidered after two years of dedicated needlework, to replace the plain hassocks which had served their purpose for too long. For the time being they would continue to serve their purpose a little longer in St David's.

Uncle Will was a fount of wisdom. I decided to visit him before I made any response to the farmer's demands. Eleanor was at the surgery. Marlene had taken Elspeth, who had been well wrapped up to cope with the cold weather, to the park opposite the Vicarage. Mrs Cooper was in the kitchen peeling potatoes and singing the inevitable Bing Crosby Christmas ditty in discordant tones. I interrupted her solo to inform her that I was going out, and to ask her to answer any telephone calls.

'I'll do my best, Vicar. I haven't done it before, you see,' she said, giving the impression that she was petrified by the challenge.

'There's nothing to it, Mrs Cooper,' I replied. 'Just pick up the receiver and say "Abergelly Vicarage". Then you make a note of who it was speaking and what message they leave.'

'Well, I will do my best, Vicar,' she said hesitantly. 'I'm not very good with such contractions like the phone.'

'Don't worry, you'll find it easy, believe me,' I assured her.

Twenty minutes later I arrived at Llanybedw Vicarage. It was a grime-ridden building suffering from the attentions of the nearby chemical works, which was belching out its yellow smoke as I got out of the car. Uncle Will had seen me through his study window and came to meet me. 'Welcome to the Llanybedw health resort,' he said and shook my hand. 'Come on in, boyo, before you get yellow fever.' Once inside his study he continued his comments on the industrial atmosphere. 'At least, it's only coal dust you get in Abergelly. I think I would prefer black to yellow.'

When we were seated and drinking cups of coffee supplied by his wife, a petite lady with a strong Cardiganshire accent who was dwarfed by her giant of a husband, I gave him an account of my phone encounter with Daniel Evans. I prefaced this with Jack Richards' description of the mishap with the piano. To say that he was highly amused would be an understatement. He laughed until the tears trickled down his cheeks. 'Fred,' he managed to say eventually, 'you are the innocent abroad. What on earth made you think you could transport a piano up that steep hill with all its bends, on the back of a clapped-out coal lorry? Now you are faced with a grasping old man who is trying to make capital out of your misfortune. You'll have to learn to dig your heels in and refuse to budge when someone like Evans Blaenymaes tries to pull a fast one. Tell him that you are going to consult the Farmers' Union about the price of sheep before you do anything about it. As for removing the mortal remains of your old Joanna, I should recruit Bevan the Coal to do that. He owes it to you for what has happened. If his tailboard had been in a decent condition the piano should not have gone through it. Use your loaf, boyo.'

After the back seat of my car had been loaded with the hassocks supplied by Uncle Will, 'each one sanitized by hand', I drove back to the Vicarage reflecting on the advice he had given me. By the time I was in my study, I had decided that I would ring up Jones, Blaenycwm Farm, a church warden at St Illtyd's in my former parish. He was as irascible as Daniel Evans but was someone whose honesty was beyond question. It meant another session of ear-shattering conversation, complicated by the fact that Evan Jones suffered from an embarrassing stammer as well as a tendency to shout into the phone as if he was calling to his dog from the other side of a field. I took a deep breath and picked up the receiver. 'J-Jones, B-blaenycwm F-farm,' came the reply in a cannonade of decibels.

'This is Fred Secombe here, Mr Jones,' I said. Before I could say any more, he burst once again on my eardrums. 'W-well, this is a s-surprise. H-how are you? I-I tell you w-what. We are m-missing you s-since you have g-gone.' Considering that Evan had been a thorn in my flesh and that his dog had bitten me badly on one occasion, it was a surprise to learn that he had missed me.

'It's very kind of you to say that, Mr Jones,' I replied. I somehow refrained from telling him that the sense of loss was mutual. 'I am ringing you to find out the price of a sheep in good condition, a sheep which you would judge to be the pick of your flock.'

'Don't t-tell me you have t-taken up f-farming, V-Vicar,' he said.

'No, Mr Jones. What has happened is that the church hall piano has killed a sheep belonging to Daniel Evans, Blaenymaes Farm here in Abergelly, and he wants ten pounds in compensation.' There was a long silence at the other end of the phone.

I continued with the conversation. 'It's a long story, I am afraid. All I wish to know is whether the money he is asking for the sheep is justified.'

There followed another long pause in which Evan was trying to come to terms with my assertion that a church hall piano could kill a sheep. Eventually he spoke. 'You are not p-pulling my l-leg, V-Vicar, are you? H-how c-c-can a p-p-piano k-kill a sh-sheep?'

'I am not pulling your leg, Mr Jones. In a nutshell, what has happened is that the piano was being transported up a steep hill on the back of a lorry and it slid against the tailboard, broke it and landed in a field where it collided with a sheep. What I want to know is whether the price of the sheep stated by Mr Evans is the right price.'

'N-no,' came the reply. 'He's t-trying to get m-money out of you, f-five pounds is all that he c-could ask f-for. F-fancy a p-piano k-killing a sheep.'

I put down the phone and sat at my desk considering my next move. Since it was Jack Richards who had enlisted the aid of Bevan the Coal to take the piano to Brynfelin I came to the conclusion that it was he who should get him to remove the wreck of the piano. It was half past eleven, which gave me half an hour before the Fish Bar would be open. I ran to the car and drove up to Jack's premises. As I emerged from my car my nostrils were assaulted by the aroma of frying fat. I was determined that it was going to be a flying visit.

He came to meet me when I knocked on the glass door. 'What's up, Vicar?' he enquired.

'Can you spare ten minutes?' I asked.

'Come on into the middle room,' he replied.

I sat down in an armchair and launched into the reason for my visit. 'This morning I had a phone call from Evans, Blaenymaes. He is demanding an excessive price for his dead sheep and wants the debris of the piano removed instantly to prevent his flock getting entangled in the broken wires of the piano. I have phoned a former parishioner who is a farmer, and it is obvious that Evans has almost doubled the price of the sheep. I shall see to that later today. The other thing is that we had better get rid of the piano before he charges us with an exorbitant fee for doing it himself. My friend, the Vicar of Llanybedw, suggests that Bevan the Coal should arrange to collect the pieces since it was his lorry which was responsible for the mishap.'

He stood there in his spotless white overalls, looking extremely embarrassed. 'I'm sorry about all this, Vicar,' he wheezed, 'but I don't think we can expect Ike Bevan to collect on his own. After all, it was a voluntary job for him. If you like, I'll have a word with him after he comes home from work tonight. If he is agreeable to take his lorry to the field, then we'll have a small working party to pick up everything tomorrow. It will have to be in daylight. So the men who come will either have to be working mornings or the night shift. Once I get the go-ahead, I'll go round about to see who I can get. I'm afraid that's all I can do.'

'That's quite a lot, Jack. Thank you once again for all your efforts. By the way, my wife has rung her father and he has promised to supply us with a brand new piano.'

'Marvellous,' he exclaimed. 'In that case, the least we can do is get together and cart away all that wreckage.'

When I returned to the Vicarage, Marlene had brought back Elspeth from the park and collected David from school. It was his first term at Danygraig Infant School and he was full of his own importance. As soon as he saw me he thrust one of his artistic masterpieces before my face. 'Look what I've done, Dad,' he said proudly.

'What is it?' I asked as I examined a riot of blue, yellow and red crayon lines and squiggles on the drawing paper.

'That's the Vicarage,' he replied scornfully. 'Look, there's your study window!'

'Of course,' I said. 'I should have seen that straightaway.'

'Miss Williams said that it was very good and she saw what it was as soon as she looked at it. Can't you see the blue smoke coming out of the chimney? Elspeth said she could.'

At that moment, Eleanor came in after her surgery and visiting calls. My son advanced upon her holding out his piece of drawing paper. 'You can see that this is the Vicarage, can't you? Daddy couldn't.'

'Silly old Daddy,' she replied. 'We'll have to get him some glasses because he can't see properly.'

'I don't want my Daddy to put glasses on his face,' lisped Elspeth. 'He's got a lovely face, haven't you, Daddy?'

'If you say so, my cherub,' I said. Eleanor gave me one of her looks.

As we sat in the kitchen and enjoyed Mrs Cooper's meal of sausage and mash, I told my wife about the morning's happenings. 'Good old Uncle Will,' she said. 'I am glad you went to him for advice. I should make a habit of it if I were you. As for that old man in Blaenymaes Farm, I should ring him this afternoon and inform him that five pounds is the maximum that you will pay him and not a penny more. And as for clearing up the piano pieces, I am sure that Jack Richards will collect enough men to do that. Bevan the Coal will be only too pleased to have them to help out, especially since his tailboard will be on his conscience. More importantly, my dear, I suggest that we pay a visit to Cardiff this afternoon to that piano place in St Mary Street and arrange for the new instrument to be delivered to the Brynfelin tabernacle. My father has asked that the bill be sent to him forthwith. If they are not willing to do that, then we have to foot the bill ourselves and he will send a cheque immediately to cover our financial loss.'

'In that case, my love,' I replied, 'it will have to come from your cheque book. My account is rapidly approaching a change of colour and pay day is a fortnight away.'

'How on earth are you going to buy me an expensive Christmas present, Frederick, if you are devoid of funds?' she asked.

'How do you know whether I have already lashed out on some magnificent gift?' I said.

'There are two answers to that,' my wife retorted. 'The first is that you have never bought me a magnificent present, and the second is that you always leave your purchases until the last minute, including the provision of a Christmas tree. I know you get a cut-price bargain by getting it on Christmas Eve, but it means a hell of a rush to decorate it, if you will excuse my English.'

'You know I don't like anticipating Christmas, Eleanor. In any case, it is much more exciting to be putting up the lights and the trimmings on Christmas Eve.'

'That's your excuse,' she replied. 'Anyway, don't let's waste time in debate. Get that phone call done and then we can get off to Cardiff.'

Evans, Blaenymaes, was not at all pleased to hear that I had consulted another farmer about the price of sheep. After five minutes' argued indignation he agreed to accept five pounds and an assurance that his pasture would be cleared of the perils of piano wires. Half an hour later we were on our way to the music shop. 'Did your father specify what kind of instrument we should buy?' I asked Eleanor.

'Apart from saying that he meant an upright piano by a reputable maker and not a concert grand, that was it,' she said. 'After that apology for a piano, even a second-hand cottage style instrument would have been acceptable. At least we shall have a new piano and a good one.'

It was at this stage in our conversation that we were flagged down by a traffic policeman standing by his patrol car. I was driving my Ford 8. I wound down my window. 'Sorry, Reverend,' said the policeman, 'but I am afraid you will have to turn back and take the Llanybedw road. There has just been a nasty accident around the bend. We are waiting for the ambulance to come.'

'I am a doctor, constable,' said my wife. 'I should think we had better drive up to see if there is anything I can do.'

'Of course, doctor,' he replied. 'They will be more than glad to see you.'

I drove off at once and about a quarter of a mile away we reached the scene of the accident. There had been a violent head-on collision between two cars, which had blocked the road completely. Two police cars were in attendance. Eleanor jumped out of the car and ran towards the tangle of metal which had been the bonnets of the vehicles. I followed her, wondering whether I would be needed to say the last rites on any of the occupants. Announcing that she was a doctor, she was taken by one of the constables to what had been the front of one of the cars. An elderly man was trapped in his driving seat, his face streaming with blood. The dashboard of the car had been driven into the driving wheel, making it impossible to extricate him.

'The Fire Brigade should be here anytime now,' said the policeman, 'as well as the ambulance. As you can see, the man in this other car has come through the windscreen and must be dead. I don't see what you can do at the moment, doctor.'

My stomach was heaving at the sight of the carnage. Eleanor went around to the other car and examined the mangled body. 'You are right, constable. He is dead.'

The next minute the Fire Brigade and the ambulance arrived in tandem. 'What a bloody mess!' exclaimed the leading fireman, 'sorry, Reverend.'

'That's exactly what it is,' I replied.

'I am a doctor,' said my wife to the ambulance men, 'but it looks as if we can do nothing until the firemen cut away the metal to get at this man. The other one is dead, I'm afraid.'

I left them and went to the dead man. Closing my eyes to shut out the sight as well as to pray, I commended him to the mercy of God. When I had finished my short prayer, the firemen unloaded cutting equipment and began to attack the twisted metal. After half an hour, the ambulance men were able to release the unconscious man and place him on a stretcher. Eleanor examined him. Blood was trickling from his mouth. His face was badly cut. 'It looks as though his lung has been punctured. His ribs are badly damaged and so is his pelvis.' In no time at all the ambulance was on its way to the casualty department.

'I don't think I want to go on to Cardiff,' I said to my wife.

'Nonsense!' she replied. 'If you will allow me, I'll drive your car. There are only a few days left before the dedication of the church. I tell you one thing. You would never make a doctor. Snap out of it, Secombe, and concentrate on your priorities.'

I sat silently as she drove to Cardiff. Constantly in my mind's eye was the mutilated body of the man who I had commended to God's mercy. He was a young man, as far as I could see. I wondered if he were married, perhaps with a young family. If that were the case, I could imagine the distress of his young wife and of his children. By the time we reached St Mary Street in Cardiff, I had invented several scenarios, all of them harrowing. Parking the car proved to be a tiresome problem. Eventually we had to go into a car park some streets away.

Once inside the premises of Cardiff's premier piano store, I emerged from my self-imposed gloom for the time being. We were invited to try the tones of several upright pianos. Since I was no pianist, I listened to my wife as she regaled herself with busking a number of Gilbert and Sullivan tunes, to the pleasure of potential customers and the annoyance of the gentleman in his elegant pin-striped suit who was anxious to clinch a sale. Eventually, to his great relief and the disappointment of the small audience which had gathered, Eleanor decided on a Challen upright.

Next came the negotiation of the sale. The pin-striped sales assistant refused to allow the piano to leave the shop until he had a cheque in his hand. My wife stressed the fact that her father was a much respected GP in a prosperous town in Monmouthshire. It was to no avail. She opened her handbag, produced her cheque book and announced that the Vicar, who was with her, could provide proof of her financial viability, as a general practitioner herself. When he saw that her signature was preceded by 'Dr', he dismounted from his high horse and began to grovel instead. 'Thank you very much indeed, Dr Secombe. When would you like the piano delivered?'

'By next Friday at the latest,' she said. 'It is needed very urgently.'

'We only do deliveries in the Valleys on a Tuesday, so I am afraid it will have to wait until next week,' he replied.

My wife's hackles rose. 'Either we have it by next Friday, or I cancel that cheque.'

The minion made a swift departure to the manager's office. He returned a few minutes later, red-faced and breathless. 'Yes, Dr Secombe, we are able to arrange a special delivery next Thursday. May I have the details, please, as to where the instrument is to be taken.'

By now it was nearing closing time for the shop. The negotiations were completed quickly and we were soon on our way back to our parked car. 'I think I ought to phone Marlene. She'll be wondering where we are,' said Eleanor.

We found a call box and I waited outside as she made her call. I could see her face show signs of concern, as she put more coins into the box. I wondered what further tales of calamity would be unfolded when she came out. Eventually she replaced the receiver with an aggressive gesture and emerged with the light of battle in her eye. 'What do you think?' she exploded. 'Bernard Evans, the locum who was supposed to do my evening surgery, didn't turn up. Betty Thomas phoned up his house and had no reply. She had to cope with a queue of irate patients who are probably blaming me for what has happened. What is more, the Health Authority will come down upon me like a ton of bricks.'

'Calm down, love,' I said. 'The Authority can't blame you for something which was not your fault. It is Bernard Evans who must answer for the consequences.'

'Knowing him and what a slime ball he is,' she retorted, 'he will say that he had no recollection of being asked to fill in.'

'I am sure that your receptionist will bear out that you had informed him,' I replied. 'If you don't mind, I shall drive back and you can sit beside me and try to relax. I don't think that we should return to Abergelly with you at the wheel in your present state of mind.'

The children had been put to bed by the time we got to the Vicarage. Eleanor was still fuming at the inexcusable dereliction of duty displayed by the man who had been asked to deputize for her. She stormed into my study and picked up the phone, dialling each number with an angry flick. I went into the kitchen where Marlene had put on the kettle to make us a cup of tea.

'Dr Secombe sounded very annoyed,' said our children's nanny.

'And so she should be,' I replied, 'and so must the patients be as well. Think how you would feel if you were in pain and needed instant attention. Anyway, how have the children been?'

'Very good, Vicar,' she said. 'Mind, they are getting very excited now that Christmas is coming. David wants to know how Father Christmas is going to get down the chimney because the chimney pots are so narrow and Father Christmas is so fat.'

'What have you told him, Marlene?' I asked.

'Well, Vicar,' she replied, 'I said that he takes the pot off and puts it on the sleigh, and the reindeers look after it while he gets down the chimney and then he brushes off all the soot with their antlers when he comes back up.'

'Ten out of ten,' I pronounced, 'and five gold stars. I would never have thought of that. I doubt if Hans Christian Andersen could have done any better.' She flushed at the compliment.

My study door was banged shut and Eleanor stamped her way into the kitchen. 'I don't believe it!' she exclaimed. 'That man had the temerity to say that he could not remember me asking him two days ago that I wanted him for the evening's surgery, and that he had no note of it in his diary. Fortunately I phoned when Betty was alongside me and she can bear witness to what happened. If anything does come of this, it is he who will have to face the music and not me. I shall never use him again, I can tell you. I am not so much concerned about the Health Authority as I am about my patients. An incident like this will soon go the rounds and I shall be known as unreliable.'

'Come off it, love,' I rejoined. 'This is the first occasion that they have ever had cause to complain. They know you well enough to realize it is not your fault.'

No sooner had I said that than the phone rang. It was a phone box call. At the other end, the caller was having difficulty with the coin box. Eventually it transpired that the lady wished to speak to Dr Secombe. When Eleanor put the receiver down, she was livid. 'That old lady was ringing to say that she had come to the surgery this afternoon to let me know that her husband was in need of treatment for his pneumoconiosis. Apparently he is coughing his lungs up and she is afraid he is on his way out. Who told me to come off it? Believe me, Fred, in my job you can't afford to have any hiccups. In yours, you can have as many as you like, but nobody dies as a result.' So saying she went into the sitting room, picked up her bag and ran out into the night.

3

It was the Friday evening before the dedication of the new church. The piano had been transported safely from Cardiff the previous afternoon. Graham Webb was attacking the instrument with a series of fortissimo chords, as the band of voluntary cleaners were engaged in preparing the building for the big day on Monday. He pronounced a very satisfactory verdict on its performance. 'Ideal for Gilbert and Sullivan music rehearsals, Vicar. Now then, apart from you and Dr Secombe, where are the other participants in the concert? I thought we were due to start at seven thirty.'

It was obvious that if he was to be the musical director of the church Gilbert and Sullivan Society he would be more of a disciplinarian than Aneurin Williams in Pontywen. As Eleanor said later, it was a distinct advantage to have a school master in charge. I was about to explain that all of the artistes on the bill had to assemble at the church hall in Abergelly, and were waiting for a hired bus to take them to Brynfelin. At that moment there was a flurry of activity outside the building which heralded the arrival of the performers.

A small committee had been set up to organize the concert. My wife and I had volunteered our services as duettists, but apart from that we had no idea of what talent was to appear on Monday evening. To my dismay I

36

noticed that Willie James, the scoutmaster, was among those who where making their way down the aisle. There was a young man with a trumpet, three young ladies in their mid-teens, an elderly man with a suitcase, and among the rest I could see Ivor Hodges' school secretary whose contralto voice he had praised. The voluntary cleaners decided to finish their work and form an audience at the back of the church.

It was a motley group who were to entertain them. Tom Beynon was chairman of the committee. He it was who had organized the bus and who was to act as compere. 'Here we are, Vicar,' he announced. 'Sorry we are a bit late. Not our fault. It was the bus. They're supposed to be a reliable firm. It looks as if they are as reliable as the council buses. Anyway, we are all raring to go, as they say. Is this Mr Webb? Pleased to meet you, I'm the People's Warden, Tom Beynon.' They shook hands. 'I've got a list of those who are going to take part,' said Tom, 'and I'll call them out in order. Not all of them will be singing, mind. Those that will be have brought their music with them. The Curate is coming as soon as he has finished training at the rugby ground.' Eleanor and I looked at each other. We had heard nothing from Hugh Thomas about his participation in the concert.

'Let's have the "Three in Harmony" first, shall we?' shouted the compere in an attempt to drown the numerous conversations. 'And what about a bit of hush to give everybody a chance to do their piece?'

The schoolgirl trio giggled their way to the piano and one of them presented Graham Webb with a sheet of music. 'It's "Walking in a Winter Wonderland",' she said shyly. The accompanist studied the score briefly and then asked if they wanted some introductory notes. They went into a huddle and decided that they would rather go straight into their routine. The giggles evaporated and they took their places on the makeshift stage like seasoned performers. It was quite an impressive copy of the Andrews Sisters, complete with gestures and earning them applause from the row of cleaners at the back. Graham gave them back their score and congratulated them. They blushed with pleasure and retreated to their seats.

'Next, William James,' said Tom. The scoutmaster came forward and stumbled over the step in front of the dais, dropping his sheets of music as a consequence. When he had gathered them together, he gave them to the pianist, announcing that he was to give a rendition of 'The Road to Mandalay'. Graham gave him a quizzical look. Willie's five-foot stature and his thick pebbled glasses were ill-suited to a musical portrayal of Kipling's British Soldier overseas. As the piano began to pound out its rhythm the soloist's basso profundo energized from the little body in a bizarre fashion. It was a good loud voice but excruciatingly off-key. As the several verses went on and on, the discordance grew so much that everybody present prayed for the end of the road to Mandalay. When it came it was greeted with silence apart from some audible signs of relief. William James went across to the piano with a strut worthy of a Covent Garden star, and collected his music after thanking his accompanist for his excellent support to his singing. He stumbled over the step again on his way back but held on to his music this time.

'The next on my list is Herbert Clement.' The elderly gentleman with the suitcase came forward and asked for a chair to be placed on the stage. He opened the case and produced a sheet of music for the pianist. 'It's "I'm Forever Blowing Bubbles" and I do this at the end of my act,' he said. Then he went back to his case and unearthed a dummy with scarlet hair and a suit which was topped with an Eton collar. The ventriloquist had a very long top lip. It met a bottom lip which had appeared to cave in under the competition from above. The result was speech which was difficult to understand when Herbert Clement was speaking in his natural voice. I wondered what would happen when his dummy came to life. To my amazement, Tommy, the wooden schoolboy on his knee, was giving lessons in diction to the man who was pulling the strings. When it came to the duet in 'I'm Forever Blowing Bubbles', every word of Tommy's contribution was distinctly heard, while Herbert's musical replies could have been in Chinese as far as his audience was concerned. It bore no resemblance to the English language.

'Clever, isn't he,' said Tom Beynon to me.

'Well, it is the first time I have ever heard a dummy speak so clearly,' I replied. 'I must say, he is a very clever dummy.'

'Now then, who's next?' said the compere, consulting his note sheets – 'Alfred Evans'. The adolescent with the trumpet came forward. He had been examining the instrument and polishing it ever since he had arrived. He was a pimply youth, with a red nose and thick eyebrows which Groucho Marx would have been pleased to sport on his countenance. 'This is Dai Elbow's nephew,' whispered Tom to me. 'He plays in the Abergelly Brass Band.'

The young man gave his score to Graham Webb. 'It's Jeremiah Clarke's "Trumpet Voluntary",' he said. Then followed a session of tuning, blowing, and emptying of spit from the trumpet. Eventually he signalled to the pianist that he was ready to begin. There was a slight discrepancy in the launch between brass and piano. Soon they were at one, and it was a splendid rendering of one of the favourite alternatives to the Bridal March. Alfred was patted on the back by his pianist at its conclusion.

'Elizabeth Williams,' called Tom Beynon. The portly lady came to the piano with a copy of *The Gondoliers*. She winked at Graham, who opened the score as if he knew what she was about to sing. The school secretary, accompanied by the music master, gave a splendid performance of the song 'On the day that I was wedded to your admirable sire' from *The Gondoliers* and sung by the Duchess of Plazo Toro. This won applause from cleaners and artistes.

Eleanor turned to me and said quietly, 'That was an audition for our Gilbert and Sullivan production, not the concert.'

'In that case,' I replied, 'she is guaranteed the contralto role henceforth. I thought Myfanwy Howells was good in our Pontywen days but she outshines her.'

Our conversation was ended by a typical Hugh Thomas entry at the back of the church. The door burst open and was closed with a bang. The next minute he was standing alongside the compere, panting as if he had run up the hill to Brynfelin. 'Am I in time for my effort, Mr Beynon?' he gasped.

'Once you have got your breath back,' said the warden. 'While you are doing that, we'll have an item by the

St Peter's handbell team.' I had wondered why Ivor Hodges was hovering at the back. He led his eight campanologists to the front of the little stage. There were four young ladies and four young men. 'We are going to play two Christmas carols,' he announced. 'I hope you will recognize them.'

Apart from a few hiccups, the team gave an easily recognizable rendition of 'O Come, All Ye Faithful' and 'The First Nowell', faltering somewhat on the grand conclusion to the second carol. Evidently it made a good impression on the listeners, who gave them a hearty round of applause.

'Is it my turn now?' asked the Curate, who had been sitting quietly, recovering his breath.

'The stage is yours,' said Tom. Hugh grinned at Eleanor and me and then informed his audience that he was going to recite the Stanley Holloway monologue 'The Battle of Hastings' – of how 'William became King of England and Harold got shot in the eye'. It was a piece that I knew well from my days in college as part of my repertoire. As he reproduced the Holloway tones impeccably I realized that here was the comic for the Abergelly Church Gilbert and Sullivan Society. He finished his performance to laughter and applause. There was no doubt that the Curate would be invaluable to me, not only as a good preacher and visitor, but also as a major contributor to the social life of the parish. Graham Webb had improvised a quiet background of music, and as soon as the monologue ended, he came across to Hugh and shook his hand. 'Excellent,' he said.

'Last of all, we'll have an item from our Vicar and his good lady.' With these words from the compere, Eleanor and I took up our positions on stage. The pianist had our copy of *The Pirates of Penzance* opened ready for our duet from the second act between Mabel and Frederick, something we had sung often on stage and for our own enjoyment at home. It was the first time parishioners in Abergelly had heard us in concert, and they proved to be very appreciative.

All in all, it was a most satisfactory rehearsal for the big day on Monday. When we returned to the Vicarage, Eleanor asked Marlene why she had not been part of the handbell team since she was a regular bellringer. 'Well, since Mr Beynon wanted the rehearsal to be a surprise for you, I couldn't very well have said that I wanted the evening off, especially as you and the Vicar were going to be up at Brynfelin,' said our nanny.

'You could have asked Mrs Cooper to babysit,' replied my wife.

'To tell you the truth,' went on Marlene, 'I would rather pull on the bell ropes than fiddle about with those little handbells.' She was a big muscular girl.

'You will have a chance to hear them on Monday,' I said, 'because we have decided to bring the children to the dedication service. We want them to be present at this big day in the Church's history in Abergelly. You had better keep it a secret until Monday afternoon, otherwise you will have to cope with our excited children who will be well past their bedtime.'

When we went to bed that night we spent an hour or so discussing the casting of *The Pirates of Penzance* instead of the future of the new church. We decided that Ivor Hodges, who did not sing that evening but who had a good baritone voice, would be Sergeant of Police. Elizabeth would be Ruth the Pirates' maid of all work. Hugh Thomas would be the comic Major General, and Willie James would be the traditional small man at the end of the line of police. We felt sure that Graham Webb would know someone who would be the Pirate King. The rest of the small parts would present no problem.

The bigger headache would be the recruitment of the chorus. Some of the choirmen at St Peter's were obvious candidates. It was the female chorus who would be difficult to recruit. They all had to be the daughters of the Major General and therefore young and attractive. There were few in the congregation of that quality. Once again we felt that Graham Webb would be the man to consult, as someone who could liaise with the music mistress at the girls' school.

At the end of all this speculation I confessed to my wife, 'I feel a nasty qualm of conscience. Here we are with a completely wrong list of priorities focused on Gilbert and Sullivan instead of St David the patron saint of our new church and the sense of mission which that entails.'

She replied, 'Think of the number of confirmations which resulted from the founding of the society in Pontywen, Frederick. Admittedly we are engaged in a piece of self-indulgence but it has its evangelical overtones.' She kissed me and said, 'Go to sleep, love, and let the Lord sort out all the implications.'

The next morning was Hugh's day off and I had to say Matins on my own. As I read the collect for the Third Sunday in Advent, with its words, 'Grant that the ministers and stewards of thy mysteries may so prepare and make ready thy way by turning the hears of the disobedient to the wisdom of the just', the qualm of conscience I had confessed last night returned with added force. Monday would see the dedication of the new church, and the following Sunday would be Christmas Day, with the first Midnight Mass in the parish. Surely here was my priority. *The Pirates of Penzance* had nothing to do with 'turning the hearts of the disobedient to the wisdom of the just'. The time and thought needed to produce the operetta would be better employed in visiting the streets of Brynfelin and using the new building as a focus of evangelical activity. I spent a long time on my knees, and left St Peter's for the Vicarage, fully determined to concentrate my heart and mind on the mission to which I had been called, with Gilbert and Sullivan in cold storage.

Eleanor was on her way out to Saturday morning surgery. I met her as she was about to get into her car. 'You don't appear to be very happy, Frederick,' she commented.

'I think we must have a long talk tonight about Gilbert and Sullivan,' I said.

'What, another one!' she exclaimed. 'We spent ages last night doing that in bed when we could have been better employed doing other things. Anyway, I have to be better employed doing other things at Brynfelin at the moment.'

She closed the door of her car and the next minute had disappeared up the drive, leaving a trail of exhaust fumes in the frosty morning air. I thought about her words, 'better employed doing other things at Brynfelin at the moment'. That was exactly what I should be doing. I should have to explain this to her later that day.

Until then I had a sermon to prepare and a visit to make to the local printer, Emrys Williams, who had undertaken to print the service for next Monday at a reduced rate. I felt it would be more appropriate to have a letter professionally produced than a home-made effort from the parish duplicator. His printing establishment was situated between a newsagent's shop and a shoe repair business, and was very similar to the one I used to visit in Swansea, when I was editor of the school magazine. The machine, with its lines of type, was situated behind the counter and its owner always wore an apron, stained with printer's ink. So every visit to Emrys Williams meant a welcome indulgence in nostalgia, an antidote to the worrying realities of the present.

'It's all ready for you, Vicar,' said the printer. 'A big day for Brynfelin. It's about time something was done for them up there. My nephew and his wife live in Glamorgan Terrace just around the corner from the new church. They will be at the service on Monday. They are both confirmed but haven't been to church for ages.'

'Let me have their names and address, will you, Emrys?' I replied. 'They sound like the kind of people who could form part of a nucleus of worshippers.'

'Oh, I don't think Gareth and Marion would consider themselves to be in that category,' he said. 'Anyway, go and call on them. They will be pleased to see you, I'm sure.'

'There's no time like the present,' I told him. 'I shall call on them this afternoon.'

I went back to the Vicarage with my package of the forms of service and immediately went to work on my sermon for tomorrow. The epistle for the day was part of the Epistle to the Ephesians, beginning with the wonderful words set to music by Purcell, 'Rejoice in the Lord always and again, I say, rejoice'. This was an anthem which I had sung several times at my parish church, both as a boy and as a young man. I consulted my Bible commentary, which informed me that those uplifting words were spoken 'in the face of trials endured, for which forbearance is needful'. I remembered Eleanor's words when I met her earlier, 'You don't appear to be very happy'. If I determined to follow a course of ministry which involved a renunciation of my delight in Gilbert and Sullivan, I should not be a rejoicing servant of God. I would become a vinegary, miserable specimen of humanity who would not inspire others with the spirit of rejoicing. I would be like a vicar I once knew at the beginning of my ministry, who forbade his congregation to visit the cinema or a dance hall in case they enjoyed themselves.

It was a bemused Eleanor who was greeted with the news that I did not want a long talk about Gilbert and Sullivan. 'You certainly look a lot happier than when I left this morning,' she said. She was even more bemused when I told her that the change had been brought about by my sermon preparation. 'God moves in a mysterious way, his wonders to perform,' she remarked.

That afternoon I drove up to Brynfelin to visit Mr and Mrs Gareth Morgan at their home in 13 Glamorgan Terrace. The door was opened by a young man, apparently in his late twenties. He was clad in an overcoat and was sporting an Abergelly rugby club scarf. 'I am the Vicar,' I announced. 'Your name has been given to me by your uncle who says that you and Mrs Morgan will be at St David's for the opening of the church on Monday.'

'Come on in, Vicar,' he said. 'Sorry I can't stop long. I'm off to see your Curate play against Neath this afternoon.' He led me into the parlour and then shouted to his wife, who was upstairs. 'We've got a visitor, love!' Mrs Morgan, a pretty brunette, appeared a minute or so later. She, too, had the Abergelly scarf around her neck. 'This is the Vicar, Marion,' said her husband.

'Pleased to meet you.' She had a pleasant speaking voice, well modulated with a slight huskiness and devoid of the valleys' sing-song accent.

'I don't want to delay your visit to the match,' I said. 'It's just that I have come to say how pleased I shall be to see you at our service at St David's. I hope we shall be able to regard you both as regular worshippers.'

'Well, Gareth and I have been having a talk and we have decided to turn over a new leaf and we shall be at Communion every week from now on. That's a promise. By the way, if you're going to get up a choir, Gareth and I would like to be in it. We both enjoy singing.'

By the time we parted, five minutes later, they had offered themselves as potential members of the Church Gilbert and Sullivan Society as well. It had been a most productive visit. I was glad to think I had taken my form of service to the printer.

It was Marlene's day off, and Eleanor had taken the children to see their grandparents further up the valley. I decided to go to Abergelly park to see my Curate play that afternoon. When I arrived at the ground play had started and chants of 'Aber, Aber' were filling the air. All seats in the stand had been taken, and I had to push my way into a reasonable place to see the match. The wearing of a clerical collar was useful for this purpose. My height of five foot seven made it imperative that I was near the front in any standing-room enclosure.

To my horror, my first sight of the match revealed that Hugh Thomas was lying on the ground, attended by the trainer and watched by an anxious team captain. I sent up a silent prayer that the injury was slight. It was a selfish petition more concerned with his necessary presence in church the next morning than anything else. My prayer was heard as Hugh sat up, shaking his head as if coming out of a nightmare. Three more doses of cold water from the sponge on the back of his neck, and he was standing upright. The trainer stared into his face for signs of concussion and then after a word to the outside half trotted off the field with his Gladstone bag. There was an outburst of clapping for the recovery. The next minute the referee blew his whistle and play continued.

I was beginning to wonder whether I had done the right thing by coming to watch the match. By half time I had become a nervous wreck. Every time Hugh received the ball I was willing him to get rid of it as quickly as possible. Since he was determined to hang on to it more often than not, my blood pressure must have reached an all-time high. I felt I had to stay until the end, having made the effort to see the game. The next forty minutes was an ordeal, somewhat mitigated when my Curate scored a solo try which brought rapturous applause from the Abergelly supporters. When the final whistle was blown, it was a moment of sweet relief.

As I made my way from the ground, surrounded by the excited spectators who had seen their team win by a single point, I met up with Gareth and Marion Morgan. They expressed their surprise at seeing me.

'This was my first visit and my last,' I said. 'I can't stand the strain of watching.'

'I know it was a nail-biting last ten minutes, Vicar,' replied Gareth, but the great thing was that we won.'

'It was not the nail-biting last ten minutes that caused the strain,' I explained. 'When I arrived I saw my Curate stretched out on the ground. I spent the rest of the match wondering whether he would be carried off on a stretcher the next time he was injured. What the eye does not see, the heart will not grieve.'

'Hugh is a tough player,' said Gareth. 'He may be short in height but he is very sturdy. A fortnight ago he laid out one of the Blaengwyn prop forwards with a flying tackle. It was worth the price of admission to see that, like the try this afternoon.'

'I take your word for it,' I replied, 'but what matters to me is his presence in church on Sunday not his prowess on the rugby field on a Saturday. As long as they do not clash, that's fine.'

It was a subdued curate who appeared in the vestry the following morning. He sported a black eye and bruised countenance. 'Sorry about my appearance, Vicar,' he murmured. 'We had a bruising encounter with Neath yesterday afternoon, as the press would put it.'

'I wouldn't need the press to put it,' I replied. 'I saw it for myself.'

His uninjured eye opened wide. 'You were there at the park?' he exclaimed incredibly.

'I was indeed. It was my first visit and my last. I spent all the time wondering whether I would have to be minus a curate for weeks or possibly months. Sooner or later you will have to decide which is the more important, Abergelly Rugby Club or the parish of Abergelly. What is the Bishop going to say when he sees your battered face tomorrow evening?' He stood quiet, with his head bowed, a most unusual attitude for Hugh Thomas. I felt a pang of remorse. 'Let me put it this way,' I went on. 'For the time being, and certainly for this season, I shall not stand in your way.'

His head came up and his hand shot out, grasping mine in a vice-like grasp. 'Thanks a million, Vicar, you don't know what that means to me.'

When I told Eleanor at lunch about the vestry conversation, she said, 'It was a safe bet that you would give in to your Curate. You make a habit of that, love.'

'Well, at least I have warned him,' I replied.

'Is that what you call a warning?' she commented. 'By the way, I hope one of his fellow lodgers will make an extensive application of her powder puff to his eyelids and cheek bones before he appears before his Lordship tomorrow.'

It was obvious that he had been given that treatment when he arrived at Evensong later in the day. He was his ebullient self once again and preached a rousing sermon on John the Baptist's words in the Gospel for the day: 'I am the voice of one crying in the wilderness.' Watched by the three admiring females from his 'digs', he thumped the pulpit and stabbed the air with his pointed finger as he proclaimed that, as from tomorrow, the church would be crying aloud in the wilderness of Brynfelin. 'Notice!' he shouted. 'I said the *church*, not just the clergy. It means you, the congregation here in St Peter's. You have an obligation to be spreading the word by joining in an evangelistic campaign of doorstep visiting and helping to make the new church a centre of social activity to attract the inhabitants of that benighted estate.'

By the time he had finished his *tour de force*, the perspiration had dissolved the camouflage of powder and he came down from the pulpit with his black eye exposed to view.

Monday dawned with lowering skies and the onset of snow. 'The last thing we want now,' I said to my wife before I left for Matins, 'is a heavy snowfall.' I should not have said that. By the time Hugh and I had finished our service there was a layer of snow on the ground and the flakes were coming down in profusion.

Eleanor was about to drive away when I came back to the Vicarage. 'I hope I can get up the hill to Brynfelin,' she said through the opened window of the car.

'You'll be able to do that, I'm sure,' I replied. 'It's tonight I am worried about. If this carries on, the two buses Tom Beynon has booked will never make it. The only way to get there will be a trudge through the snow, believe me.'

My pessimistic forecast proved to be correct. By six o'clock the skies had cleared and the moon was shining on an arctic landscape where traffic in the Valley had ceased to operate. Tom Beynon called to say that the bus company had informed him of their inability to provide transport. As he sat in my study, the telephone rang. It was the Bishop.

'My dear Fred,' he said, 'I am so sorry that I cannot possibly get to your parish. Like everybody else apparently, I am stranded. I would suggest that you postpone the dedication until next Thursday evening when I am free. If you want to go ahead with the dedication, do so by all means. However, it would be a great pity if the inauguration of a new place of worship, so badly needed, was attended by only a handful of people.'

'I am most grateful to you, my Lord,' I replied. 'To go ahead with the service would be a pointless exercise. I think most of our congregation and the people on the estate must realize that we could not possibly go ahead with the dedication. Thank you once again. I am sure that in a couple of days' time the weather will have relented.'

'I know one person who will be glad for the postponement,' remarked Eleanor a little later that evening.

'And who may that be?' I asked.

'Your Curate, of course,' she replied. 'By then his injuries will be apparent no longer.' Any further conversation was prevented by the ring of the doorbell.

When I went to the door I was confronted by the sight of Willie James against a background of snowflakes. He was clad in a thick overcoat which was supplemented by a pair of wellingtons, most of which were submerged in the depth of snow around the doorstep. A bobble hat covered his head as far as his spectacles. He carried a suitcase in his gloved hand. 'I've been up to St David's,' he said, 'but it was locked up.' He turned away and looked up at the sky through his snow-flecked glasses. 'It's started again,' he continued. 'I suppose it's because of the snow that there's no service. I thought I'd better come and enquire in case there were other arrangements.'

'There are indeed, Willie,' I replied. 'The dedication will take place next Thursday evening, same time, same place. I am sorry you had a wasted journey. You had better come in and have something to warm you up before you go home. You must be all in.'

He removed his spectacles and brushed the snow from his eyebrows. 'If you don't mind, Vicar, I think I had better get back before it gets worse. Thank you all the same.'

I watched him plough his way towards the gate, clutching his suitcase to his bosom like an antarctic explorer who had lost his team of huskies.

As his diminutive figure disappeared, I felt I should have insisted that he came into the Vicarage for a respite before his journey home. 'Who on earth was that?' asked Eleanor when I came into the sitting-room.

'Willie James,' I said. 'He had climbed all the way to St David's only to find the place locked up. By the way, he was carrying a fair sized suitcase. He looked exhausted.'

'I should think so,' she replied. 'Why on earth didn't you ask him in, poor little man?'

'I did, but he said he wanted to get back, in case the snow engulfed him completely I expect. You see, there's a blizzard raging outside. I wonder what was in the case,' I remarked.

'You will soon find out next Thursday,' said Eleanor. 'Perhaps you will find that he has changed his act to ventriloquism. That will be much more interesting than "The Road to Mandalay".'

4

By Thursday the snow had cleared from the roads but there were the remains of snowdrifts in the fields and gardens, waiting for more to come, as my mother would say. The weather was bitterly cold, with a penetrating north-easterly wind afflicting anyone who dared to go outdoors. David and Elspeth were confined to their playroom and were causing Marlene considerable harassment by their excitement at the prospect of Father Christmas paying them a visit in a few days' time. As Mrs Cooper remarked, 'They are giving her Mary Ellen. Still we can't say anything, can we? I'm sure we were just as constrepuous when we were their age.'

I was downstairs in my study, closeted with Hugh Thomas, whose face had healed fortuitously in time for the Bishop's appearance at the dedication. 'By the way, Vicar, I met Jack Richards on my way here. He told me to let you know that he has had the electric heaters on all night to prevent a freeze-up of the pipes in the kitchen and to warm the church ready for tonight.'

It was at this stage in our conversation that the phone rang. 'Bishop here,' said the voice at the other end. 'Just to confirm that I shall be at St David's this evening. However, I am afraid that I shall not be able to stay for your festivities after the service. I think it would be unwise to prolong my visit in case the roads become too icy for safety. I hope you don't mind, Fred, but I am sure you will appreciate my concern. In any case I have a very busy day ahead of me tomorrow which requires an early night for me.'

After I had thanked him for ringing me, I suggested to Hugh that we should go up to Brynfelin to check on the preparations for the evening. When we arrived at the church, not only was Jack Richards there but a number of ladies who had brought cakes and sandwiches for the post-dedication celebrations. The excitement of expectation was even greater that that which prevailed in my children's playroom. It was infectious. Both my Curate and I were carried away on a tide of enthusiasm.

Dai Elbow arrived, having come off the night shift in the colliery. As he came through the door he was singing in a very loud voice 'Oh! What a beautiful morning!'

'That's a matter of debate, Dai,' I shouted.

'Don't be like that, Vic,' he said, as he came down the aisle. 'I know it is like the arctic outside but it's our great day, isn't it. By the way, it's a great day for you, too, Vic. Remember those raffle tickets you bought for the Christmas Draw for the Workingmen's Club. You've won a chicken. Eddie Harris will deliver it to the Vicarage this afternoon. It's a prime bird, 'e says. Anything I can do to 'elp?'

'Yes,' replied Jack Richards from the kitchen. 'First, stop singing and second, come down here and have a look at this boiler that we've borrowed from the hall. It doesn't seem to be working. I thought I'd try it out ready for tonight but it's not heating the water at all.'

''Ave you looked at the plug?' enquired Dai.

'Of course I have,' retorted the honorary works fore-man. 'I'm not that daft.'

'Just asking,' said the electrician. 'Must be the element in that case. I'll 'ave a look now once I get my tools from the car. I tell you what. If that's the case, you'll 'ave to get a boil-er from somewhere else.' His prognosis proved to be correct.

Next came the problem of finding a water heater at short notice. As we sat in a huddle, scratching our heads and trying to think of a likely source of succour, Dai slapped his leg and shouted, 'Got it!'

I stared at him. 'Come on then, let us have it.'

'The Workingmen's Club. Eddie 'Arris is going to bring you the chicken this afternoon. 'E can bring you the boil-er at the same time. I'll go down there straightaway and find out if they're willing to lend it for tonight.'

'Look, Dai,' said Jack Richards, 'if you are going down there now, why don't you bring it back with you, rather than waiting until this afternoon? The sooner it's up here the better!'

'Quite right mun,' he replied. 'I know 'Arry Brown, the steward, quite well. We used to play together for Abergelly. Good prop 'e was. A bit dirty, mind.'

Coming from someone who had been banned perma-nently for foul play, it was the extreme example of some-one who had shattered a glasshouse, daring to criticize someone who had thrown a handful of gravel. Jack blew his nose loudly and then looked up at the heavens. The Curate and I maintained a discreet silence. 'Won't be long!' he bellowed as he went through the door.

'That takes the biscuit,' exclaimed the fish and chips merchant. 'Harry Brown was an angel compared with him. Anyway, what matters is that he comes back with that heater.'

The catering committee finished their preparations and made their way out in an explosion of animated conversation. Half an hour later the door was opened and Dai Elbow came in backwards holding the boiler in his brawny arms as if it were a scrum half he was trying to strangle, out of the sight of the referee. 'Got it!' he announced in stentorian tones for the second time that morning. He performed an about-turn and paraded the water heater triumphantly down the aisle.

When I went to the Vicarage for lunch, I informed my wife about the generosity of the Workingmen's Club. 'Without them,' I said, 'we should have been in an awkward position. Not only that but very soon we shall be the recipients of another outpouring of their Christmas goodwill.'

'What on earth do you mean?' asked Eleanor. 'It sounds as if *you* have already been the recipient of a generous outpouring of Christmas goodwill.'

'Nothing of an intoxicating nature has passed my lips,' I replied. 'Dai Elbow has told me that I have the winning ticket for the prize of a chicken in the Club's Christmas draw. He sold me five tickets a week or so ago. It seems that Eddie Harris, the secretary, will be here this afternoon with what is apparently a prime bird.'

'Prime bird or not,' she said, 'it will be a very welcome addition to our Christmas fare. It can bide its time in our new fridge.'

We were relaxing in the sitting-room after our meal when there was a ring on the door bell. As I went to the porch, I could hear a squawking noise outside. When I opened the door, I was confronted with the sight of a chicken, its two legs tied together, being held upside down, its wings flapping frantically and its vocal cords creating a cacophony. It was in the charge of an embarrassed little man, impeccably dressed in a dark overcoat and a grey trilby. By now I had been joined on the doorstep by my wife. 'With the compliments of the Workingmen's Club, Vicar,' he stammered. He deposited the protesting bird on the lawn and, as fast as his legs could carry him, hurried away to his car, which was parked at the entrance to the drive.

We stood in silence, nonplussed by the bizarre presentation of our Christmas prize, which was lying exhausted after its protestations. Eventually I said to Eleanor, 'Do we release it into the wild or do we condemn it to the fridge?'

'And who is to carry out the sentence of death if it is the second course we adopt? I can't see you doing that. As for the first course, there is no such thing as a wild chicken. It looks as if I shall have to put it out of its misery before the children come to find out what is happening.' She went straight to the hapless bird. Before it could register any further protests, she seized its neck and twisted it. 'That's put it out of its misery, poor thing,' she said. 'And now we must get Mrs Cooper to remove its feathers. As for it being a prime bird, by the look of its legs it has been walking around the farmyard for quite a time. I should think it passed its prime long ago.'

She carried the corpse into the kitchen, as I tagged along behind her, still in a daze after the events of the last few minutes. Mrs Cooper, who was at the sink, turned around and gazed wide-eyed at the sight of the feathered fowl.

'I am afraid our prize has come with all its clothes on,' explained Eleanor. 'Do you think you could pluck it for us?'

'Well, I've never done it before,' was the reply, 'but I'll 'ave a go, Joe, as Wilfred Pickles used to say. Perhaps you could show me the mechanicals of it, Dr Secombe. Once I've got the hang of it I'll be off like greasy lightning.'

Five minutes later, with newspapers spread out on the kitchen table, my wife gave a demonstration, and true to her word our daily went to work like 'greasy lightning', watched by our fascinated children, who had just come down from their playroom. As Marlene said, 'Thank God for the chicken. They were just beginning to go over the top.'

At six thirty prompt, the Vicarage family plus Marlene crammed into Eleanor's car and we made our way to Brynfelin ready for the service at seven thirty. The icy blast had intensified with nightfall. As we disembarked on top of the hill, in Masefield's words, the wind 'was like a whetted knife'.

Inside the prefabricated building there was a hive of noisy activity as helpers from the parish church were making last-minute preparations. The rattling of cups and saucers in the kitchen was almost drowned by the hubbub of conversation. At the piano the music master, Graham Webb, from Ivor Hodge's school was indulging himself with a *mélange* of Christmas music. I had forbidden the decoration of the church until Christmas Eve so that the austerity of Advent should be observed. There may not have been any decoration, but Advent had taken second place to the feast of the Holy Nativity, which had already arrived in St David's, in sound if not in sight. A steady flow of parishioners and post-dedication artistes began to fill the building. However, as Hugh Thomas observed, 'everybody seems to be here except the people for whom the church is intended'. When the Bishop arrived some twenty minutes before the service was due to start, there was not a single person from Brynfelin in the congregation.

His Lordship, his thin sallow face sporting an incongruous red nose, had driven solo. He complained that the heater in his car was not working and that he was 'chilled to the marrow'. The chill soon evaporated as he entered the warm bath of crowded humanity inside the new building, where the temperature had already been raised by Jack Richards' twenty-four hours' heating. By the time he had robed in the close confines of the vestry, the Bishop's forehead was sprinkled with small beads of perspiration. 'What an exciting time for you and your people,' he remarked. 'The establishment of a new outpost in God's Kingdom. Before long, God willing, there will be a permanent church dominating the hill, as the present parish church dominates the valley.'

I had no desire to pour cold water on the episcopal rhapsody by mentioning that none of the hill people were in church so far. I kept my tongue firmly in my cheek.

Out in the church Graham Webb was playing his piano version of what I know as Bach's 'Sheep may safely graze'. We had decided not to transport the harmonium from the church hall in case there was a further slaughter of sheep on the Blaenymaes farm. In view of its absence, the church organist decided that he would leave the accompaniment for the service to the school music master. As Eleanor remarked, 'That means there should be a decided improvement in the singing, since the congregation will not be competing with Evan Roberts.'

When we emerged from the vestry for the service, I searched for signs of fresh faces amongst the worshippers. To my great delight I could see Eddie Roberts and his widowed mother. He was a young man who had been at death's door for months after a motor bicycle accident on Brynfelin. I had visited him assiduously in Abergelly hospital. Both mother and son had promised they would be faithful attendants at St David's when it was erected. Now there he was, seated in the front row with his crutches on the floor at his feet and his mother at his side, beaming proudly at me. At least here were two people who lived on the hill. 'Upon this rock,' I said to myself, 'I will build my Church, if you will excuse my plagiarism, Lord.' I had decided on the hymn, 'Guide me, O, Thou Great Redeemer' as the opening act of worship. It was one of the few occasions when it could be said that I was deeply moved by music in which the lungs of the singers had joined forces with their hearts.

The Bishop dedicated the church, the altar and the little wooden font carved out of oak by Ben Davies, one of the construction team. The dedication was done in between the verses of 'We love the place, O God, wherein thine honour dwells'. Hugh Thomas read the lessons with his usual panache. The Bishop's sermon was addressed to the people of Brynfelin and their obligation to bring others into the congregation of St David's, a mighty task for the only two inhabitants of the housing estate present. As soon as the service was over, his Lordship disrobed quickly and went out into the night to his unheated motor car, anxious to return to his home comforts and above all the warmth of his centrally-heated residence.

Meanwhile, inside the newly dedicated building, preparations for the celebratory concert were in progress under the guidance of Tom Beynon, while cups of tea and plates of sandwiches were being dispensed by the lady helpers. David and Elspeth were being fussed over by several old ladies, who competed with each other for their attention. They must have been asked at least a dozen times what they wanted from Father Christmas. What with the noise of the handbell ringers practising their routine, the tinkling of the piano as Graham Webb was giving a run-through to some of the soloists, and the torrent of conversation, the noise was becoming unbearable. I decided to go outside for a minute's peace and breath of fresh air.

To my dismay, as I opened the door I was met by a flurry of snowflakes. I closed it quickly and went down to tell my wife that it looked as if a blizzard had begun. 'I had better drive Marlene and the children to the Vicarage,' she said, 'and then come back up before the road gets treacherous.'

'In the meanwhile,' I replied, 'I think I'll have a word with the Wardens about the concert.'

I called Tom Beynon and Ivor Hodges together for a quick assessment of the situation. 'It would be a pity if we called off the concert only to find it was just a snow shower,' said Tom, who was anxious to parade his artistes.

'On the other hand,' Ivor pointed out, 'it could mean that the grand finale of the evening would be incarceration on a snowbound mountain.'

'What we need,' I suggested, 'is a look-out.'

'Dai!' shouted Tom Beynon, 'come by here a minute.' Dai Elbow had been introduced to the Bishop, together with Jack Richards and other members of the construction team. He had addressed the prelate as 'Your Worship', and was as full of pride as if he had been presented at Buckingham Palace.

'Anything I can do to 'elp, Tom?' he enquired.

'Could you sit outside in your car for half an hour or so?' said Tom.

'Wot in the 'ell for?' asked Dai.

'The Vicar says it has started snowing. If it keeps on getting thicker all the time, we'll have to finish the concert and get everybody out before we get stranded up here,' came the reply.

'I'll go and get my coat now,' he said. 'I've got a flask of 'ow's-your-father in the inside pocket. So I'll be able to keep off the cold.'

'For God's sake,' warned Tom, 'don't have a drop too much and fall asleep. Come and tell us straightaway if it has stopped or if it looks as if it's in for the rest of the night. Now then, Vicar, let's get the concert going. If it's only a few items it's better than none.'

I made a short speech in which I thanked the construction team for all their hard work, and the ladies of the parish for their excellent catering. 'Now I shall hand you over to Tom Beynon who will compere the concert for this evening.' This was the signal for Willie James to hurry to the vestry with his suitcase.

The three young ladies who did their impersonation of the Andrews Sisters singing 'Walking in a Winter Wonderland' were warmly applauded. 'Now we come to the next item by Willie James. He is going to sing "On the Road to Mandalay".' When the scoutmaster emerged from the vestry, his weedy little figure dressed in his scoutmaster's uniform and a home-made topi on his head, the audience collapsed in laughter. To say that Willie was disconcerted by this reception would be an understatement. He stood blinking at them through his jam-jar spectacles, apparently unaware that the pianist was repeating the introduction without any response from the soloist. He came out of his trance after Graham Webb's third attempt to get the solo going, singing loudly off-key, which produced more amusement. However, as the never-ending verses continued, amusement turned to boredom and his listeners passed the time in conversation to such an effect that the last line in the song announcing that 'the dawn comes up like thunder outer China cross the bay' was inaudible against the chattering background.

It was at this juncture in the proceeding that the door at the back burst open. My wife and Dai Elbow made a joint entrance, both of them bearing evidence that the snow, like Eliza, had come to stay. They made their way to the front. 'If you want to get back to Abergelly tonight,' proclaimed my wife to all and sundry, 'you had better remove your vehicles immediately.'

The bus driver, who had brought a full complement of parishioners, was the quickest off the mark, followed by the more opulent members of the congregation who had brought their cars.

Willie James stood mesmerized on the makeshift stage, apparently waiting for the applause to follow his act. Meanwhile Graham Webb had abandoned the piano, leaving the scoutmaster as the sole occupant of the east end of the church.

Mrs Roberts and Eddie remained seated at the front. I pushed my way through the throng and told them that they would be given a lift home once the chaos had subsided. Tom Beynon appeared alongside me. 'Well, I've heard of the gold rush, Vicar, but this is the first time I've ever seen a snow rush.'

Blasts of cold air invaded the warm building through the open doors, causing a drastic drop in the temperature. By now Willie James had retreated to the vestry and emerged with his case, into which he must have bundled his best suit, not waiting to change, his spindly bare legs exposed beneath his overcoat. 'They won't go without me, will they, Vicar?' he pleaded in tones of panic.

'I'm sure they will do a head count and since you were the last person to occupy the stage they won't forget you and your performance,' I replied.

As he joined the rear of the exodus, Eleanor, who had been into the kitchen to collect some trays we had lent the catering committee, joined the People's Warden and me. 'That was a fantastic example of a quick evacuation in case of fire. At least twenty people must have escaped through the kitchen door, carrying their impedimenta with them. I have now closed that exit,' she said.

'Well,' I replied, 'there's just one more evacuation we have to make and that's Eddie and his mother.'

'Don't worry about us, Vicar,' said Mrs Morris. 'We

only live just around the corner. We were waiting for all that scramble to be over. We went out in the snow last Tuesday. Eddie's crutches just go right down into the snow. There's no danger of him slipping or anything.'

'That's right,' added her son. 'We'll be fine.'

'You may be fine, Eddie,' said my wife, 'but you will find it very cold outside. I insist that you come with us, in our car.'

'How about you, Tom?' I asked. 'Ivor has taken his bellringers in his car. Jack Richards has taken a crowd in his car.'

Tom replied, 'I thought I'd stay behind and lock up. It won't take me long to walk down. I've done that kind of thing many a time in the past.'

'That time is long past,' said Eleanor firmly. 'If you wait here, we shall come and pick you up once we have transported Eddie and his mother.'

When we came out a few of the cars were still revving up their engines ready to depart. The snow was being blown into us horizontally in the raging easterly wind, and by the time we reached our car we looked like peripatetic snowmen. Eddie stayed in the car when we reached his home, while his mother battled her way to the front door with the key clasped in her hand and pointed like a dagger in the direction of the lock. 'Vicar,' he said, 'if you want anybody to help in St David's, I'm your man. Once I get on my feet properly, I mean.'

'Thank you Eddie,' I replied. 'I tell you what, you shall be my server at communion. I shall be starting confirmation classes next month. You must come to them.'

'I'll be there first in the queue,' he said. He picked up

his crutches and then made his way up the path into the house.

As we went back to the church to rescue Tom Beynon, my wife remarked, 'There's your right-hand man in St David's and believe me, you will not have a more loyal supporter than that young man.'

The journey downhill to Abergelly was a nightmare of skids, and snow attacking the windscreen. I was glad that it was my wife at the wheel. When we dropped Tom at his home, he said, 'Well, my dear, you are not only a good doctor and Vicar's wife, but you would make a good rally driver as well.'

'Thank you, kind sir,' she replied, 'but I'll stick to life in the surgery and at the Vicarage if you don't mind. One more journey like that and I would be a nervous wreck, I can tell you.'

When we awoke early next morning the snow had stopped and the moon looked down on an arctic waste. The gale force wind had given place to a quiet calm. It looked as if we were to have a sunny day. 'I hope the roads are clear for the Midnight Mass at St David's,' I said to Eleanor, 'otherwise we shall have an empty church. I thought we would have seen that couple I visited who said they wanted to worship at the new church. Like everybody else in Brynfelin, they were conspicuous by their absence. Our only hope is that the advert we have put in the paper announcing the Midnight Mass will bring a few people.'

'Why don't you ring the *Gazette* to see if they would give you coverage in the news section as well as the advertisement columns,' suggested my wife. 'I thought they would have sent a photographer and reporter to the

Dedication Service. They can atone for that by plugging the first Midnight Mass to be held in Abergelly.'

'In an Anglican church, you mean,' I replied. 'Father Joe would be most insulted to read that.'

Father Joe McNally was the Roman Catholic priest in charge of St Francis of Assisi, a small red-brick church in the back streets of the town. He and I had been friends ever since he had approached me to get permission to celebrate Mass in the daughter church in Pontywen, as there was no place of worship for his people in the town. The Bishop had allowed the use of the church, and Joe's gratitude knew no bounds. When I came to Abergelly he was one of the first to visit the Vicarage to welcome me. Before I rang the *Gazette* I thought I would ring Joe to let him know that he had a rival service at midnight.

I waited some time for an answer. Eventually the phone was picked up and the housekeeper's voice greeted me. Miss Murphy was an aunt of his, 'several times removed', as he put it, and an excellent cook, as I could testify. 'St Francis of Assisi,' she announced in the tones of County Antrim.

'Miss Murphy,' I said, 'Fred Secombe here, could I speak to Joe, please?'

There was a pause and an intake of breath. 'I'm afraid, Reverend, that he has been taken to hospital last night. They say it's a very bad stroke. He can't speak at the moment and he's paralysed down his right side. He's in Ward 7 in the hospital if you want to see him.' Her voice faltered.

'I'm so sorry, Miss Murphy,' I replied. 'I shall see him this morning some time.'

Eleanor was about to go to surgery, and was opening the garage door, standing in a few inches of snow. 'If you want to be of help, Frederick,' she said, 'come and get the spade from the garage and clear away a path down the drive.'

'Before I do that,' I replied, 'I have some bad news. Joe McNally has had a severe stroke. He is in hospital unable to speak and is paralysed down his right side.'

She stood staring at me. 'When did this happen?' she asked.

'Last night, apparently,' I said. 'Poor Miss Murphy sounded dreadfully upset. It isn't as if he were just another priest. After all, he is family. I said I would go and see him later this morning.'

'I'll try and find out more from the hospital when I'm at the surgery,' she replied, 'and I shall let you know.'

I took the spade from the garage and began to vent my emotions on the snow.

'Steady on, Secombe,' she ordered, 'otherwise you will be ending up with him in Abergelly Hospital. That's enough clearing away, thank you. I suggest you go back to your study, sit on your posterior and ring the *Gazette*.'

I was put through to a sub-editor of some kind. 'I am afraid we are snowed under, if you will pardon the pun. That is the reason we were not able to cover the dedication of your church. However, if you can give me a few details about the service last night plus something about your Midnight Mass, I'll see what I can do for you.'

When I put the phone down, Hugh Thomas arrived, having acted as chauffeur to his three fellow lodgers and his landlady. 'With all that female flesh crammed into my little car it's a wonder I made it down that snow slope,' he said. 'I felt convinced that we would end up with the sheep in Evans Blaenymaes' field. That we arrived at Raglan House safely can only be attributed to the power of prayer. Now then, Vicar, what are we going to do to get the inhabitants of Brynfelin to church for the Midnight Mass? As far as I can see it will be another case of St Peter's congregation filling St David's.'

'You will be pleased to know that the *Gazette* are going to do a piece on the dedication, with a postscript about the first Midnight Mass to be held in the parish of Abergelly in the new church,' I replied. 'Whether that will produce a result we shall have to wait and see.'

'What about a rush order of leaflets?' he suggested. 'We could have them printed today and get help to deliver them tonight and tomorrow?'

'In that case, Hugh,' I replied, 'you had better get down to the printer's and order a thousand. I'm afraid I have to pay a hospital visit. Father McNally has had a severe stroke.'

'That's a shock,' said my Curate. 'He looks a picture of health. Father Joe is someone who could well be playing for our team.'

'It seems that he will not be playing for any team for some time. Let's hope it is a temporary absence, not a permanent one.' With those words we parted.

The council lorries had gritted the main roads, and my Ford 8 had no trouble making its way to Abergelly Hospital, where the car park's surface had not been treated. As a result, when I had locked my car, and strode towards the entrance I slid a few yards and landed on my back, to the amusement of two young nurses who were on their way to the wards. Their amusement turned to concern as I found myself unable to get to my feet. The next minute I found myself being gently brought to a horizontal position sandwiched between the two.

'Are you all right, Vicar?' enquired one of them.

'Apart from a loss of dignity,' I said, 'and a slight bump on the back of my head, I feel OK.'

'Let me have a look at your head,' she ordered in professional tones. She examined my head, which was still ringing from its impact with the ground. 'As you say,' she pronounced, 'there is the beginning of a lump which will grow in size before long, I should think. I'll tell you what, we'll take you to casualty for a check-up.'

'That's very kind of you,' I replied, 'but I don't think there is any serious damage. If I feel any worse after I have visited Ward 7 I shall call in there on my way out.'

'If you are going to Ward 7,' said the other nurse, 'you can have an escort because that is where we are going. I expect you want to see Father McNally.'

'I do indeed,' I replied.

'Well, you will be pleased to know that before we came off duty, he was beginning to speak. You will be able to see for yourself.'

When I was ushered behind the screens, I was greeted by the welcome voice of Father Joe. 'Fred,' he managed to say out of the side of his mouth. I sat down on the chair which he indicated with his left hand. His right arm was lying inert on the bedclothes. To see a man who abounded with energy a prisoner of paralysis was a sight I found difficult to bear. I decided to speak to him as normally as I could. I told him about the dedication of the church and our troubles with the snow. After a few minutes his eyes began to close. I caught hold of his left hand and squeezed it. 'See you next week, Joe,' I said. He did not hear that. He was asleep. As I left his bedside, the Sister came behind the screen. 'He's asleep,' I whispered. She looked at Joe, went across to him and felt his pulse. 'I'm afraid, Vicar, that is the sleep of death,' she said. 'I think you had better go while we attend to him.'

5

Not until I sat down in my armchair in the study did I realize that I had seen someone's last moments on earth for the first time in my life. It was such a quiet passing. No pain, no struggle, just a peaceful process of surrendering one's soul into God's blessing. I wished that my departing would be like Joe's. Then I thought how privileged I was that the last word he had spoken was my name. I recalled the happy times we had together, with Joe playing the piano while we sang our favourites from *Ancient and Modern*, the only opportunity he had to do so. 'I think I'll have to compile a selection and teach them to my people,' he had said once. 'The only difficulty will be the harmony. They always rely on the organ to do that while they sing everything in unison. I think that will be an uphill struggle, but worth it. One day you may hear the strains of "Cwm Rhondda" echoing around St Francis of Assisi, with the basses and tenors raising the roof. That's just a dream of course.'

My reveries were ended by the ring of the telephone. It was Eleanor. 'The latest update at nine o'clock this morning on Father Joe's condition, is bad, I'm afraid. Apparently the stroke is a major one and there is little hope for him. Have you been to see him yet?'

'Well, my love,' I said, 'I can give you a more up-to-date bulletin. I was at his bedside when he passed away half an hour ago. It was such a wonderful end that I thought he had fallen asleep. I had the shock of my life when the Sister came in, felt his pulse and then told me he had just died.'

'All I can say,' replied my wife, 'is that such a good man deserved a good end. You will miss him, Fred. He would have been another "Uncle Will" for you, and there are not many more around like that.'

'I am still trying to come to terms with what has happened,' I said. 'Next time I read the burial service sentence "In the midst of life we are in death" it will mean a lot more to me than just a phrase. I've seen it for myself.'

'I must ring off now,' she replied, 'much as I would like to talk more. The surgery is still full of patients. See you at lunchtime.'

When I put the phone down, I became aware that my head was reminding me that it had come into violent contact with the hospital car park. My lumber regions joined in the reminder with a painful ache. As I stood up, my legs registered a further protest. I thought of the Paul Robeson record of the song from *Show Boat*, 'body all aching and racked with pain', and was glad I did not have 'to tote that barge and lift that bale'. However, I did have to face a mountain of activity to prepare for the Midnight Mass at St David's, and the Christmas services in St Peter's. I went slowly upstairs to the bathroom to receive comfort from a bottle of aspirins in the medicine cupboard – each step adding to my discomfort. Sounds of riotous merriment from the nursery greeted me as I reached the landing. I loved my children dearly, but to say that I was out of tune with their excitement, would have been an understatement.

I opened the bathroom door and made my way to the cupboard.

The next thing I knew, I was on the floor with an audience of Marlene and Mrs Cooper looking down on me. 'Stay where you are, Vicar,' ordered our 'daily'. 'Dr Secombe is on her way down. She said that with no account must you be allowed to move from by where you are.'

'To be honest, Mrs Cooper,' I breathed, 'I don't think I could if I wanted to.' I found it very disconcerting being watched by an ashen-faced young amazon and a red-faced, grey-haired, whippet of a woman, both of them at a loss for words. The pain in my head and body was excruciating. 'Marlene,' I managed to say, 'do you think you could get me some aspirins and a glass of water, please?' There was a banging on the nursery door. 'Perhaps you had better go and see to the children first, Marlene,' I said.

To my intense relief I heard the front door open. The next minute Eleanor was at my side, out of breath but full of anxiety. 'Hello, love,' I croaked, 'can you give me a painkiller, please?'

'Before I do that,' she replied, 'can you tell me what has happened?'

'I slipped on the snow in the car park at the hospital and fell and bumped my head,' I said.

'Why did you not tell me that when I phoned you?' she asked with a certain amount of vehemence.

'I didn't think I'd hurt myself,' I murmured.

'You've got delayed concussion, my dear,' she said, 'and you will have to be X-rayed, once I think you are fit enough to move.'

Half an hour later I was back at the hospital. Because my wife was in the trade, as it were, I had instant attention. The X-ray showed no harmful effect from the fall. As we drove back to the Vicarage, Eleanor said, 'I have never known a man as accident prone as you are. Take it easy for the rest of the day. I'll get back to the surgery where the natives must be very restless by now.'

I lay sprawled across the settee in the front-room for a while. Marlene was back upstairs with the children, and Mrs Cooper was busy in the kitchen. I fell asleep only to be awakened by a ring on the door bell. Our 'daily' sped down the passage to open the door. It was Hugh Thomas. Mrs Cooper and the Curate had a whispered conversation.

'Come on in, Hugh,' I shouted. He poked his head around the door.

'I was told you were not to be disturbed,' he said quietly.

'That does not apply to you,' I replied. 'Sit down for a minute. There is so much to be done. I think I had better give you a list of priorities.'

He produced his pocket-book from his pocket. 'If you don't mind, Vicar,' he said, 'I shall have to borrow a pen or pencil from your desk.' He was back in the armchair in no time at all, his pencil poised. 'Fire away. Oh! before you do that, I've come to tell you that the printer says the handbills will be ready by five o'clock.'

'Fine,' I said. 'Number one priority is to see that they are distributed around the estate tonight and tomorrow. At least the weather is better now, that's something. However, it's one thing to have good weather, it is quite another proposition to arrange the distribution.'

'What about the scouts?' he suggested.

'My dear Hugh,' I replied, 'most of the leaflets would end up making paper darts or be hidden behind garden walls, if they were given the job. In any case, they are not meeting until after Christmas. Not only that, but they would have to be transported to Brynfelin. I would suggest that you ask for volunteers when the working party meets to decorate the church tonight. By the way, you can ask the printer why his nephew and his wife did not turn up for the dedication service. Apart from Eddie and his mother they are the only direct contacts we have up there. When I visited them, they said they would be keen to be part of the congregation and help in any way they could. The name is Mr and Mrs Gareth Morgan, 13 Glamorgan Terrace. Perhaps you could give them a call this evening.

'Number two on your list, will you check with Tom Beynon this afternoon about the Christmas tree? He knows someone in the Forestry up at Llanafon. It's supposed to be delivered at seven o'clock this evening. Dai Elbow has got hold of some fairy lights, and he will be fixing them. James the Greengrocer's are supplying the tree for St Peter's as they have done for donkey's years. Number three, would you mind taking three bottles of wine from the crate in the vestry at St Peter's before you go up to Brynfelin? I took a box of communion wafers there yesterday. I think that's all for the time being.'

'Any more, Vicar, and I would have writer's cramp. By the way, I have arranged to have in bold headlines at the top of the leaflet "Put the Christ back in Christmas in Brynfelin". Then underneath "Come to the first Midnight

Mass to be held in the parish at your own church of St David". I'll see myself out. I shan't bother you any more today. Hope you'll be better by tomorrow.' The next minute there was a roar of the engine and his MG was skidding its way up the drive.

I went back to sleep and did not awake until Eleanor arrived back home after surgery. 'I think you had better phone the Rural Dean,' she said, 'and ask him if he can find someone to stand in for you over Christmas.'

'Not on your Nellie!' I shouted. 'After all the effort I have put in to get that church erected, to have someone else celebrate at the first Communion Service to be held there – no way!'

'Calm down, Frederick,' she replied. 'If you are not fit tomorrow morning and I shall decide that – you will not be allowed out of this house. If you don't phone old "Shall I say", then I will. Even should you be able to take the services, at least you will have covered yourself. You can't expect him to get hold of a replacement at a moment's notice.'

Very reluctantly and trying to hide the discomfort of my aching body, I rose from the settee.

'For someone who claims he will be fit tomorrow,' my wife commented, 'that was hardly the leap to action of someone who was raring to go. You have had a nasty fall.'

I made my way to the study and dialled the Rural Dean. 'Rural Dean speaking,' came the pompous rely.

'This is Fred Secombe, Mr Rural Dean.'

'Oh! yes, Vicar,' he said.

Perhaps I should have described myself as the Vicar of Abergelly, I thought.

'Well, Vicar,' he went on, 'what is it I can do for you? That is, if I can, shall I say.'

'This morning when I was visiting the hospital, I slipped on the frozen snow and had a nasty fall. As a result I am suffering from delayed concussion and I don't know whether I'll be fit enough to take my Christmas services. I was wondering whether you could warn a priest to stand by just in case?'

Evidently this recital of events and their consequences was taking some time to be absorbed by the dignitary. It was quite a while before there was any sign of life at the other end of the telephone.

'I am very sorry to hear about your being invalided as it were. Well, as far as getting someone to help is concerned, my hands are tied up, shall I say? I would suggest that you get in touch with the Archdeacon. He has a list of retired clergy and such like. I'm sure that he will be able to find someone to fill up the bill for you, shall I say.'

When I told Eleanor of the Rural Dean's response to my request for help, she said, 'I should have known better than to advise you to get in touch with him. I wonder what locum will be provided by the Archdeacon, whether it will be someone from the list of retired clergy or from the list of such like?'

The last time I had to ask the Venerable Griffith Williams for help was during my incumbency in Pontywen. On that occasion he sent me an elderly gentleman with bladder trouble, who had to make frequent visits to a receptacle placed in the vestry, to the puzzlement of the congregation. It seemed that every time there was a hymn he disappeared. I hoped the Archdeacon would produce somebody from his list of 'such like'. When his monotonous parsonic tones greeted my call I sent up an arrow prayer for assistance. The Lord heard my call.

'Well, Vicar,' he droned, 'you are most fortunate. At Christmas time, there is always a scarcity of available clergy. However, only this morning I had a phone call from the Bishop informing me that his newly appointed chaplain would be on hand to help out with any emergency over Christmas. I would suggest that he comes to you in any case, even if you feel better tomorrow. His name is Michael Hunt, Michael Hunt, and his phone number is Llanybont 225, Llanybont 225. I think you should phone him straightaway. He will be at home lunchtime. Llanybont 225, and his name is Michael Hunt. I hope you have got all that.'

'I have indeed, Mr Archdeacon, and thank you very much for your help,' I replied.

I had not noticed my wife standing behind me. 'It has worked then!' she exclaimed.

'Don't startle me like that,' I said.

'Your nerves, Frederick!' she replied. 'Now then, what did he say and is the stand-in coming from the "such like" list?'

'He is, you will be pleased to know, and his name is Michael Hunt repeated in triplicate together with his phone number in triplicate,' I said.

'Well, my dear, you do that in reading the banns. It is obviously a good ecclesiastical practice. Anyway, who is Michael Hunt?' she asked.

'None other than the Bishop's newly appointed chaplain, to quote the Archdeacon, and I have to phone him straightaway,' I said. 'Furthermore he *has* to come here and not act as a standby.'

'Thank God for his venerableness,' she breathed. 'Now then, do what he says and get on that phone. I promise I shall not be behind you. I am going to help Mrs Cooper get our lunch ready. By the way, do you know him?'

'I know him,' I replied, 'but I have never met him. He was ordained at the same time as Barney Webster.' Barnabus Webster was a 'mature' candidate for holy orders who was assigned to me as a curate in Pontywen and proved to be a disaster. 'If you remember,' I went on, 'he read the Gospel at the ordination service.'

'Oh, that young man,' she said, 'good looking and full of charisma. Aren't you lucky?'

I rang Llanybont 225 and the call was answered almost before the dialling tone had time to announce itself. 'Michael Hunt here,' proclaimed the voice at the other end.

'This is the Vicar of Abergelly. I understand from the Archdeacon that you are available to help out in an emergency over Christmas. I am afraid I had a nasty fall this morning and as a result I am suffering from delayed concussion. I have a Midnight Mass in our newly erected daughter church, and three services of Holy Communion at 8 a.m., 9.30 a.m., and 11 a.m. at the parish church. The Curate, who is a deacon, will preach at the 11 a.m. service.'

After a brief interval he returned to the phone. When he had taken down all the details, he said, 'I know how to get to your parish church but you will have to give me directions to your daughter church.'

'I think it would be better if you came here to the Vicarage,' I replied. 'My wife will take you to St David's

Brynfelin, and if I feel fit enough I shall come as well, even if I cannot take the service. You see, it is the very first eucharist in this church and I should hate to miss it.'

'I shall be honoured to be the first celebrant, Vicar,' he said. 'If I am with you by 11.15 p.m., will that be all right?'

'Splendid,' I replied. 'We shall be pleased to offer you hospitality in between the services on Christmas Day. I am most grateful to you for your help.'

I put the phone down and went into the kitchen where Eleanor was laying the table. 'It's all fixed,' I announced. 'I have told him to come here on Christmas Eve and that you will transport him to Brynfelin. Furthermore that we will provide him with hospitality between the services on Christmas Day. Oh! and I did say that if I felt well enough I would come up with you to St David's.'

'Did you indeed?' she replied. 'And who will be looking after the children? Marlene will be back at Pontywen with her Mum and Dad for Christmas.'

'Excuse me, Dr Secombe, said Mrs Cooper. 'If you want me to babysit I'd be only too pleased. I shall be spending Christmas on my own. I hope you don't think I'm too presumptive, butting in like this.'

'Not at all,' replied my wife, 'you can spend the night in Marlene's room and, if you want to, spend Christmas Day with us.'

Our daily's face beamed with pleasure. 'Thank you very much, I would love to be with you all. It would make my Christmas.'

That afternoon I was ordered to bed by my resident doctor, who was about to go on her rounds. 'If you stay on that settee, you will be tempted to be up and about when you should be resting,' she said. I was given some sleeping tablets to give my brain a rest as well as my body.

Unfortunately they were not dream-preventative tablets. It was six o'clock when I awoke, after a nightmare which left me sweating with apprehension. I dreamt that St David's had been set alight and that all that remained of the building was an empty shell containing the smoking ruins of its interior. It was so vivid that when Eleanor came into the bedroom, I was still in a state of shock.

'What's the matter, love?' she enquired.

'Would you believe it?' I said, 'I have just dreamt that St David's has been destroyed in a fire.'

'So much for the tablets,' my wife replied. 'According to the blurb which accompanied them, they were supposed to guarantee oblivion. Either you are an exceptional case, which, knowing you, is more than likely, or in ordinary mortals they are quite effective. In any case, my love, you had better come downstairs. Your dinner is ready. Marlene and the children are waiting for their food. I warn you that there is a high degree of excitement since our nursemaid will be going back to Pontywen tonight and she is just as keyed up as the children.'

When I rose from my bed, I was delighted to find that my headache had disappeared and that the ache in my back and limbs was considerably diminished.

'If I am like this tomorrow,' I told Eleanor, 'I am sure I can take my services.'

'Wait and see,' she replied.

The next morning the improvement continued. 'I'll ring Michael Hunt,' I said at the breakfast table, 'and tell him that his help is no longer required.'

'What a pity!' Eleanor remarked. 'I was looking forward to driving such a good looking and charming young man to Brynfelin.'

'It's just as well that I have recovered,' was my reply.

'Vicar, you are a real old spoilsport,' she said.

I rang the Bishop's chaplain, who insisted that he would still like to come to St David's. 'Super!' exclaimed my wife when I came back to the kitchen with the news.

The front door bell was rung with the typical Hugh Thomas flourish. 'Good looking young man number two,' said Eleanor. My Curate was full of *joie de vivre*. Evidently all had gone well at St David's, the previous evening. 'How are you Vicar?' he asked. 'I must say you are looking ten times better than yesterday afternoon.'

'I am much better and I shall be able to take the services, thank God. Furthermore we shall be having the additional assistance of Michael Hunt, the Bishop's new chaplain.'

'Great!' said my Curate, 'I know him quite well. He was in the last year at University when I began as a fresher. He was President of the Union.'

As he plunged himself in the armchair in my study he launched into an enthusiastic account of the events at Brynfelin. 'By this afternoon,' he announced, 'all the leaflets will have been distributed in Brynfelin. Mr and Mrs Gareth Morgan will have done most of them. They are a smashing couple, keen rugby fans. The reason why they were not at the dedication was that it was her parents' golden wedding anniversary. They did turn up in the snow on Tuesday only to find the church locked up. Some of the decorators who were there last night have taken the rest of the leaflets. The church looks very colourful, loads of holly and the tree is quite a big one, the top touching the roof. Dai Elbow has done a fine job with the lights. Jack Richards has bought some Christmas roses for the altar. I have taken the communion wine to the vestry. By the way, I have brought a couple of the leaflets for you to see.'

He put his hand into his overcoat pocket and produced the advertisement for the service at Brynfelin. 'Put the Christ back in Christmas' proclaimed the lurid red letters at the top of the leaflet. Then followed, 'Come to the first Midnight Mass to be held in the parish of Abergelly. 11.45 in your own church of St David. Next Sunday 11 a.m. Holy Communion. Very shortly Sunday School will begin in the afternoon. Youth Club during the weeknights, women's meetings on weekday afternoons. A men's club once a month. Something for everybody.' At the bottom in large letters, 'St David's has arrived and like Eliza has come to stay'.

'Very impressive, Hugh,' I said, 'but tell me, on whose authority does this list of organizations appear?'

His face reddened. 'What I thought, Vicar, was that we had to offer something attractive, not just that bald state- ment that there was to be a Communion service at mid- night. You were far too busy doing other things, and I felt that we had to fill up the leaflet with a worthwhile programme.'

'In that case,' I replied, 'you will have to bear the brunt of this, rugby training or not, and please don't ever do anything like this without consulting me first. You shall have the responsibility for Brynfelin, by all means, but only on condition that you come to me for permission. Is that clear?'

'Perfectly clear,' he said quietly, 'and I apologize for jumping the gun.'

Later that morning Marlene bade us farewell before she went to catch the bus to Pontywen. Her excitement at spending Christmas at home was tempered by the thought that she had to be without the company of Elspeth and David for that time. She hugged them and kissed them as if she was leaving them for ever. Elspeth was tearful but David was dry-eyed. Since he had begun attending school he was much more self-reliant, whereas my young daughter was seldom apart from Marlene. Eleanor had closed the surgery until after Boxing Day but of course was available for emergency calls. 'Let's hope the Lord will do a locum and leave me to enjoy our Christmas in peace,' she said.

I went across to St Peter's to visit the decorating party there while my wife was engaged in doing the Vicarage decorations, including the adornment of the tree which I had planted in a bucket of soil from the garden. The children were busy 'helping', which was proving to be a hindrance which Eleanor could have done without. Mrs Cooper was in high spirits in the kitchen, anticipating spending Christmas with us in the Vicarage.

When I arrived in the parish church, I found just a handful of ladies and they were not busy about the place but forming a little knot of conversation in the middle of the aisle. The tree from James the Greengrocer's was lying on the floor at the foot of the chancel. There was an entire absence of joyful anticipation of the morrow. As soon as they saw me they indulged in a dyspeptic bout of complaints that St Peter's was being neglected in favour of

St David's. 'Where's everybody?' was the cry. To my great relief Tom Beynon appeared. 'Come on, girls,' he shouted as he came down the aisle, 'I expected to see half of the church decorated by now.'

Mrs Evan Roberts, the organist's wife, emerged from the group as the self-appointed spokeswoman. She went up to Tom and poked him in the chest. 'There are just five of us here, as you can see,' she said acidly. 'We have always been at least a dozen. I suppose all the others were up at Brynfelin last night.' Apparently Eirwen Roberts was a friend of Mrs Amos Perkins, widow of the church-warden who had been a large thorn in my flesh. I had the impression that she had been affronted by my invitation to the music master at Abergelly Secondary Modern School to preside at the piano for the opening of St David's.

'Now come off it, Eirwen,' replied Tom. 'I'm sure there will be some more ladies coming. Perhaps they have to do their Christmas shopping before they can be free to join you. My wife for one. She'll be here in half an hour or so. Now, look, the last thing we want is a split between St Peter's and St David's. They need all the help they can get up there. Ivor Hodges will be here in a minute and we'll have that tree up in no time. I brought down a load of holly last night. So what about spreading it on the win-dows. You'll find plenty of greenery in the vestry, together with the holly. So let's get going!' The organist's wife glow-ered at him. The rest made their way to the vestry to begin their work.

Tom turned to me. 'Nice to see you, Vicar,' he said. 'We were worried about you at Brynfelin last night. The Curate said that you might not be able to take services over Christmas after the fall you had up at the hospital.'

'I'm fine now, thank you, Tom,' I replied. 'All the more so for seeing you. You turned up just at the right time. There was a touch of the Amos's a minute ago.'

'Don't worry about that,' he reassured me. 'Eirwen Roberts is not in the same league. Those days are over.'

Half an hour later the scene was transformed. Ivor Hodges had arrived in company with Dai Elbow. In no time at all, the tree was in position, the fairy lights were twinkling, and holly decorated the window sills with the occasional vase of white chrysanthemums. Best of all was the Christmas crib, which Ivor's pupils had created with puppet figures of Mary and Joseph and the shepherds. 'They have made three excellent wise men,' he said, 'but we shall keep them in reserve for the Epiphany.' All was at peace in St Peter's.

When I returned to the Vicarage, I found Hugh Thomas getting out of his car and looking very worried. 'Vicar!' he exclaimed, 'I have just been up to St David's. There has been a break-in. They have taken the lights off the Christmas tree. The wine has gone from the vestry. Jack Richards' flowers have gone from the altar. The communion wafers were strewn all over the floor. They used one of the candles from the altar to provide them with light. So there is candle wax everywhere. Some of the chairs were knocked over. It looked a real mess when I put the lights on.'

'Have they done any damage, written any graffiti or anything like that?' I asked.

'No, thank God,' he said.

'In that case, we can get us some lights for the tree. A visit to James the Greengrocer's will get us some flowers.

There is plenty more wine down here. How did they get in?'

'They broke the window in the kitchen. So that will have to be repaired,' he said.

'Come over to the church with me and we'll have a word with Tom and Dai Elbow,' I told him.

The news of the break-in came as a shock to the decorating party. Dai Elbow's language was unfit for Christian ears. Eirwen Roberts was the only one who claimed not to be shocked. 'I'm not a bit surprised. I tell you what. This is just the beginning. You're wasting your time up there.' I had to restrain Dai Elbow, who was so incensed at her words that he looked as if he were about to administer a physical rebuke. When we left the church arrangements were in hand to replace the missing items, including a pane of glass, for the kitchen.

'No man having put his hand to the plough and looking back is fit for the Kingdom of God,' I quoted to Hugh.

'Quite right, Vicar,' he replied. 'We are totally committed, aren't we? Mrs Roberts was probably right in one way. I expect the building will not escape further invasions. But a waste of time, never!'

As Eleanor said when she heard the news, 'Well, at least they did not burn the place down, as you dreamt, my dear. Petty thefts are nothing. The church is still there and that's what matters.'

6

I could not believe my eyes when I entered St David's at
11.30 p.m. There had been a number of people outside
when the Vicarage car arrived, bringing my wife, myself
and the Bishop's chaplain. Inside the building was a congregation almost filling every seat and with still a quarter
of an hour to go. Dai Elbow and Gareth Morgan were giving out hymn sheets and prayer-books. Evan Roberts was
wheezing carols on the harmonium. Hugh Thomas was
lighting the candles on the altar. There was scarcely a face
from St Peter's to be seen. These were Brynfelin inhabitants. It was an excited band of worshippers whose level
of conversation was almost enough to drown the organist's efforts.

There was a big smile on Dai Elbow's face as he came
up to me. 'Marvellous, isn't it, Vic?' he said.

'Marvellous?' I replied. 'It is absolutely incredible. I
didn't think those handbills could produce such an effect.'

Dai looked at me in a conspiratorial way, tapping the
side of his nose. 'It wasn't the handbills. It was the rumour
somebody started on the estate. They think your brother
is coming and is going to sing something in the service.'

I turned to Gareth. 'Is this right?' I asked.

He nodded his head. 'It has been all the talk today,' he
said. 'I didn't contradict it. If that is what is going to bring
them here, I thought, that is all that matters.'

'That is not the point,' I replied. 'When they find out that he is not here they will want their collection money back as a refund. What is more, they may start a riot, shouting, "We want Harry!"'

The Bishop's chaplain intervened at this point. 'I don't think they will do that, Vicar. As this gentleman has said, at least they are inside the four walls of the church for the first time. I am sure that you will be able to say something in your address which might take the edge off their disappointment and point the way to their involvement with the church in future.'

When Michael Hunt and I went into the vestry, Hugh Thomas was in a state of exaltation. 'Fantastic, isn't it, Vicar? Whoever would have thought that the good people of Brynfelin would have filled the church for the first Communion Service to be held here.'

'That is what I have been telling your Vicar, Hugh,' said Michael. 'Whatever may have brought them here, at least they know what the inside of the building looks like. They can see the Christmas tree lit up and the decorations of holly and ivy about them, they will realize that the church is not a dreary place.'

'Thank you both,' I replied, 'but I am not a spellbinding preacher. Even if I were, I am sure that would not be enough to compensate for their disappointment. I don't suppose, Hugh, that you may know who has been responsible for starting this rumour about my brother being here?'

'All I can say in answer to that, Vicar, is that Dai Elbow was up here when I arrived with a look of highly pleasurable anticipation on his face. "I've got a feeling this church is going to be full tonight," he said. 'If I were you I wouldn't say anything to him. It is his effort at evangelism. Flawed it may be, but effective.'

'Thank you for your advice, Hugh,' I said coldly, 'but you must leave that to me. You don't have to lie to evangelize.'

There was a full-throated rendering of 'O Come, All Ye Faithful' to begin the service. When I stood in front of the altar to deliver my first sermon in St David's church, I was conscious that it was one of the most important moments in my ministry. I waited for the conversational murmurs to die away before I began to speak.

'First of all, may I wish a very happy Christmas to you and your families. It is in the family that this festival is centred. I know that so many people say that Christmas is for the children. It is not. It is for mothers and fathers as much as for their children. The home at Nazareth was much more important than the stable at Bethlehem. That is where Jesus was brought up and taught the meaning of the love of God and his fellow men. This church of St David's is here for you and your families. Here you can worship together and your children can learn to know why Jesus came down to earth on the first Christmas Day. You will go home from here tonight and fill pillow-cases with the Christmas presents you are going to put at the foot of their beds. The best Christmas present you can give them is to fill their hearts with the love of God. You can't buy that; even if you had all the money in the world. I am told that many of you were under the impression that my brother was coming to this service. He is far away from here in Barbados with his wife and family. I am sure he will be remembering the Christmases of our childhood. The pillow-cases were not over full in the days of the Depression, but the love of our parents was more than adequate compensation for that. May God bless you all and may this first Christmas service in St David's be a beginning to a fuller and better life for you and your children. Amen.'

The reception of my 'few words' was not encouraging, to say the least. There was much unwrapping of sweets and a low murmur of conversation. When I mentioned my brother's holiday in Barbados, a large lady in the front said, 'It's nice for some, isn't it?' The collection plates brought to the altar had a preponderance of copper, with a few sixpenny bits to provide a *soupçon* of silver. As Hugh Thomas, Michael Hunt and I stood waiting to administer the sacrament, we had to witness a large exodus of members of the congregation. In the end twenty-five communicants was the number entered in the brand new register in the vestry. The only two from Brynfelin were Mr and Mrs Gareth Morgan.

When we unrobed, I said to Hugh, 'So much for Dai Elbow's ploy, Mother is it worth it?'

'Come on, Vicar,' replied my Curate. 'If you remember I told the PCC before we opened the church that it needs only one or two dedicated Christians to form the foundations, then we shall have to build on that. Gareth Morgan and his wife are very enthusiastic. They covered ten streets giving out handbills. There's the rock on which to build the church in Brynfelin. Then don't forget we have Eddie Roberts and his mother.'

The Bishop's chaplain turned to me and said, 'What's more, Vicar, if you don't mind my saying so, you are well blessed to have such an assistant. I am sure that once he is priested next Petertide, and he has that much more authority, he will be able to turn St David's into a church rather than a prefab.'

I felt chastened. The feeling intensified as Eleanor drove us back to the Vicarage. 'How wonderful to see a full church for your first Communion Service in Brynfelin. I know hardly any of the locals stayed for communion. That means that they were not confirmed anyway. From what you say they were probably there because of a confidence trick by Dai Elbow, but at least they appeared inside the hallowed walls. So be thankful for small mercies.'

Mrs Cooper had a tray of cups of tea and mince pies ready for us when we arrived. Michael Hunt made his apologies and left immediately, ready to return later for the parish church first Communion, at which I had invited him to celebrate. 'I've not heard a sound from upstairs,' said our daily. 'I've peeped in once or twice but they are fast asleep. I must say, they are lovely children. No trouble whatsoever, a real joy ride.'

'That's the first time I have heard that our children have provided somebody with a joy ride,' remarked Eleanor later on, 'especially since they were completely inert. The poor old girl doesn't seem to have much pleasure living on her own, and I suppose that is the only way in which she could express her thanks for their company, even if it was of the silent variety. What do you say to us offering her the job of housekeeper? Before long Marlene will be wanting to spread her wings, and in any case once Elspeth goes to school there will be nothing left for her to do. I have been thinking about it for some time.'

'I say Amen to that,' I replied. 'It will be like having another edition of Mrs Richards, except that Mrs Cooper's cooking is better, even if her malapropisms are not up to the Richards standard.'

The services at St Peter's were well attended and, as the Bishop's chaplain remarked, the full altar rails compensated for the paucity of communicants at St David's. He left us to drive to his parents' house for his Christmas dinner. 'Now there's a young man who's going to be a big noise in the Church in Wales,' said Eleanor as we watched his car go down the drive. 'Not an atom of pomposity, a basinful of charisma and on top of all that more than his fair share of good looks.'

'I do believe you are smitten,' I replied.

'If I were ten years younger and unmarried, I might be,' she said, 'but as it is I am more than satisfied with what I have.'

Then she gave me a bear hug and a kiss, which was ended by David coming through the open front door with his brand new scooter which he wanted to try out. He in turn was followed by Elspeth who was carrying her baby doll. 'She wants to see David on his scooter,' she lisped. The appetizing smell of roasting turkey was pervading the hall, and for the first time for weeks I felt at peace with the world.

Jane Cooper was a war widow. Her husband, who had been a territorial army soldier for years before war broke out, had been killed in the Normandy landing. Now in her late fifties, she lived in a terraced cottage on a hillside overlooking Abergelly. It was a lonely life since she was childless and her only relative was an aged aunt in

Aberystwyth. She had been more than grateful for her work in the Vicarage to supplement the inadequate pension from the War Office. Small, thin and unprepossessing, she had a high colour which Eleanor had diagnosed as due to high blood pressure and for which she had to take a daily dose of tablets.

That high colour intensified after our Christmas dinner when Eleanor asked her if she would like to be our housekeeper and live in. It was accompanied by a flood of tears. After she had wiped her eyes and blown her nose loudly, she said, 'I'm sorry to be such a miserable joyful on Christmas Day, but it's the best Christmas present I've ever had. Oh, I'd love to keep house for you both, I would indeed, really.'

It was decided that after we had made one of the large bedrooms ready for her, she would move in early in the New Year. The children were delighted. From time to time they would be under her feet in the kitchen but 'Auntie Cooper' seemed to welcome the intrusion. Having no children herself, she was only too glad to be part of a family, even if it were an adopted part.

On New Year's Day I had a telephone call from the Archdeacon. 'A Happy New Year,' he intoned. 'It could be a very happy new year for you, I should imagine, a very happy one.' I waited for the third 'very happy' but the dignitary contented himself with two. 'I have been in conversation with Canon Edwin Morgan this morning and he tells me that he has bought a house in your parish for his retirement, which is due in February. As I am sure you know, he is one of the best-known parish priests in the diocese and has still, how shall I put it, plenty of petrol left in his tank. He knows about the task facing you in Abergelly and he tells me that he will be more than willing to help you. If you care to give him a ring …' There followed his number in triplicate. As this was included in his potted C.V. in the diocesan handbook it was a piece of superfluous information – at which the Archdeacon excelled.

'Thank you for letting me know, Father,' I said, deliberately avoiding a grovel to his rank. 'I shall phone him later today.'

I put down the receiver and went into the kitchen where Eleanor was in earnest conversation with Mrs Cooper and Marlene who had just arrived back from Pontywen. 'Sorry to break up the party ladies,' I told them, 'but I have some news to impart to my wife.'

She looked at me with eyebrows raised. 'What is it, dear?' Her tone of voice indicated annoyance at my chauvinistic intrusion. 'Top secret?' She followed me into the study and closed the door. 'Don't do that again, Frederick, that was very rude. Not only rude but positively Victorian, returning them to the level of servants. Now then, what is this news you have to impart?'

'My humblest apologies,' I replied. 'Scout's honour, I shall not repeat my high-handed invasion of the kitchen. I have just had a phone call from the Archdeacon informing me that Canon Edwin Morgan is retiring and will live in Abergelly. Apparently he is more than willing to help in the parish.'

She stared at me in silence for a moment. 'So that's all?' she said frostily. 'I thought at least you had been awarded a canonry. In any case, isn't he that pompous old fogey who likes the sound of his own voice? I was engaged in acquainting Marlene with the fact that she was going to have a fellow inhabitant at the Vicarage, a delicate diplomacy since she has enjoyed sole rights up until now.' So saying, she made a grand exit, closing the door behind her with a loud bang which echoed in the hall.

The winter's chill prevailed throughout lunch, with Marlene unusually silent and with Mrs Cooper making vain attempts at conversation. Eleanor made no contribution to a thaw in the atmosphere. The only saving grace was the babble of talk from David and Elspeth which raised the temperature from time to time. I was only too pleased, when the meal was over, to escape into my study. I picked up the diocesan handbook and turned to the page on which Canon Edwin Morgan's career was recorded.

His age was seventy-five. He had been curate in three parishes before his first incumbency in Llanafon, a place of Siberian exile in temperature and remoteness. There he remained until he came back into civilization as Rector of Cwmtwyn, a small mining town further down the valley, population, 3,500, where he had remained until his impending retirement. It was rumoured that when he was about to leave Llanafon, which had three small churches in its total population of 1,200, a young curate who had been offered the living came to see him for details of what was involved in the ministry there. 'Now then,' said Edwin Morgan, who had an impediment in his speech, 'there are three churchesh to look after. Sho on a Shunday you have to work out a shyshtem of coping with the shervicesh. I have worked out thish notish which I have placed outside the three churchesh. As you can shee, there ish no trouble for the firsht four Shundays of the month. Now then, the problem ish the fifth Shunday. When that comesh, what are you going to do? I thought about thish for shome time and then found the anshwer. Here it ish: Shervicesh ash arranged from time to time.' This was the man who was coming to 'help' me in Abergelly.

One other story told about him was his sermon on the Sunday after the death of King George the Sixth. His normal sermons lasted at least half an hour. When he began his peroration to a full church, he spoke about the beloved king for twenty minutes. His congregation heaved a sigh of relief. Then he put his hand inside his surplice and pulled out a pile of paper. 'Now then,' he said, 'and now for my shermon.' His listeners wilted at this announcement. It was said that several people left the church to make sure their joints in the oven were not burnt sacrifices, and that those who were left were in a stupor by the end of the sermon, half an hour later.

It would be very convenient to have someone to take the Communion Services at St David's until Hugh Thomas was priested. On the other hand, if his sermons were inflicted on the long-suffering few in the next six months, even that handful of worshippers might depart, leaving him with an empty church. Before ringing him, I had to decide on the right approach to his request.

I sat at my desk, pondering over my dilemma. In the end I came to the conclusion that I would make it obvious that I would only need his help on rare occasions once my Curate was priested. I had arranged the time of the service at St David's for eleven o'clock in order that I could dash from the half-past-nine service at St Peter's to get to Brynfelin. If I allowed him to take the service on alternate Sundays, and asked Hugh Thomas to preach every time, then it would be a guarantee that there would be no fall off in numbers and I would have a break from a heavy routine.

I picked up the phone and dialled the Cwmtwyn number. 'Sheven five sheven,' came the reply. Not only did Edwin Morgan suffer from an impediment in his speech but this was accompanied by a strong West Walian accent. 'This is Fred Secombe, Vicar of Abergelly,' I said.

'Thank you for ringing,' answered the Canon. 'I have been waiting to hear from you. The Archdeacon hash told you I am coming to your parish to retire. He shaysh that you will need help at Brynfelin shinsh your Curate is still a deacon. Don't worry, I'll take over the church for you for the time being. I don't want to get rushty. If you want me to preach at the parish church or take a shervish there, I'll be only too glad to do sho. Any help in vishiting the shick and that short of thing, I'm at your shervice.'

'That is very kind of you Canon,' I replied. 'I think the Archdeacon must have over-emphasized my need of help. My Curate is a very active young man and is already making his mark on the Brynfelin estate. He is an excellent preacher and an assiduous visitor. I have arranged my services to enable me to celebrate Holy Communion at St David's at eleven o'clock each Sunday. It would be of great assistance to me if you were able to celebrate every other Sunday until Hugh is priested. He will come with you and preach. Brynfelin is going to be his sole responsibility. So the more he is in church there, the better.

After his priesting, it will only be the rare occasion when I shall need help, during holiday times for example. I can only say that having someone like you in the parish will be a great advantage.'

There followed such a long silence that I felt he had put the phone down and left the room. 'Hello!' I said. 'Are you there?'

'Yesh indeed,' came the reply. 'It sheemsh the Archdeacon wash mishinformed. I thought you would have been glad to have my ashishtansh ash a Canon and shomeone with a lot of experiensh. Well, there will be plenty of othersh who will be only too pleashed to call on me for help.' This time the phone was put down with an emphatic click.

The study door opened, my wife came in and put her arms around me. 'Sorry, love,' she murmured and kissed me. 'It's that time of the month and I over-reacted.'

'You are not the only one,' I said. 'You have a companion in Canon Edwin Morgan.'

'Ugh!' she exclaimed. 'No thank you! In any case I shouldn't think he suffers in that way.'

'Hardly!' I replied. 'He offered his services to take over St David's, to preach in the parish church and even to do "shick" visiting. When I told him that any help I needed from him was minimal, he put the phone down. I was not rude and in actual fact, I thought I was very diplomatic.'

'It is just as well, Frederick, that you have made that plain from the start,' she said. 'If anyone could be calculated to put a damper on things, he would be a prime candidate. The only snag is that you are going to have him living in the parish.'

'There's one good thing about that,' I replied. 'He can't be on the Parochial Church Council because he is a clergyman. Thank God for that rule.'

'Still,' she went on, 'he can cause quite a lot of trouble, especially if he got in tow with the widow of your former churchwarden or even with the wife of your parish church organist. I would advise you to keep an eye on him. That little man could be a thorn in your flesh.

'By the way, I think we will have another kind of trouble with Marlene. She has not taken kindly to the idea of Mrs Cooper as a flatmate. It may be that we will be looking for a new nanny before long. I think she has met up with an ex-boyfriend in Pontywen, from what she was saying earlier on. It will be a pity if she goes because Elspeth dotes on her. We'll see.'

We did not have to wait long to see. Later that week our nursemaid announced that she was going back to her home town to live with her parents, and that she had prospects of working on the assembly line in a new factory which was opening there. She would stay with us until Mrs Cooper came to live in – 'She'll be able to look after Elspeth for the time being till you find someone else,' she said. It was quite apparent that she had no intention of staying in the Vicarage once her solitary status ceased to exist, despite the love she had for our daughter. However, as Eleanor said, our children had come to love Mrs Cooper in the space of the few months she had been with us. Since it would not be long before Elspeth would be going to school, it would be no great inconvenience. During those three weeks before Marlene left, we prepared our daughter for the parting. The little girl became reconciled to the loss, especially since 'Auntie' Cooper was coming to live with us and would look after her.

The following Monday we held the first Parochial Church Council of the new year. Now that the building at Brynfelin was open, it meant that we could turn our attention to the renovation of the church hall and of St Peter's church itself. There had been murmurs of discontent in the parish church congregation over the concentration of effort on St David's. The time had come to give the mother church its due place on the agenda for 1955. Above all, if we were to achieve all we wished to do it was essential to find ways and means of raising the necessary money. A sub-committee had met twice to discuss the problem. They had balked at the idea of planned giving, a new concept which had been introduced into a few parishes in England from across the Atlantic, professionally run by a commercial organization. The giving was based on the idea of the tithe, a tenth of our income going to the church. I had suggested that it might be given some thought, but such a violent attack on the pockets of churchgoers was rejected out of hand.

Instead, apart from a general appeal to raise the level of giving, it decided to recommend to the Council the talent scheme which was gaining popularity in the Church of England. Under it, members of the congregation would attend a service at which a sum of money would be handed out to individuals who would undertake to use their talents to multiply that amount several times over. They would be given six months to respond to the challenge based on the parable in St Matthew's gospel. It tells of a man with several servants who was going away for a long time, and who entrusted his money to his staff in various amounts to use to his advantage while he was away. All of them did as he requested except the one to whom he gave the least. When the others presented their lord with double the money he had given them, the servant who had received the least amount gave it back to his master unaugmented. He claimed he had hidden it in case it was stolen. He was condemned to outer darkness. As Tom Beynon said, 'I can't think anyone in the congregation would dare to do that. Even if you put it in the Co-op Bank at least you would have the interest from it.' So it was decided unanimously to adopt the scheme, and the sum decided upon was one pound.

The scheme became a big talking point among the congregation. It reached even beyond the borders of the church and was the subject of an article in the local press. 'Private Enterprise in St Peter's' proclaimed the headline. It applauded 'the initiative of the innovative young vicar who is already making his mark in Abergelly'. On the second Sunday after Epiphany the distribution of the pound notes took place during the Family Communion Service, after the money had been blessed at the altar. Ivor Hodges had suggested that there should be a hundred notes waiting for the volunteer entrepreneurs. 'It would be a dreadful anticlimax,' he said, 'if people came up to the altar, only to find that they had nothing to multiply.' As it was, there were fifteen notes left after the ceremony.

A reporter from the *Monmouthshire Gazette* was at the service and interviewed some of the participants. Dai Elbow informed him that his greyhound had improved in form recently and that all the prize money it made over the next six months would be given to the church. 'What if it doesn't win?' he was asked.

'I always cover that possibility by placing bets on the other runners,' he said. 'I tell you what, I'll see that the Vicar gets a good return.'

Others said that they would use the money by exploiting whatever skills they had, from cake-making to the sale of sketches of the parish church by an amateur artist.

As Eleanor read the report in the newspaper, she said to me, 'I know someone who will make capital out of Dai Elbow's means of raising money from his greyhound racing, Canon Edwin Morgan. I should not be surprised to find a letter in the readers' column from that pious person.'

She was right. In the following edition, there appeared a letter from him. 'I was astounded to find an item in tonight's newspaper in which it was said that greyhound races were to be used to contribute money to a church's funds. Who was it who overturned the tables of the money-changers in the Temple? If this is the approach of the clergy of today to fund raising, then it is a pity that they do not do more to multiply what is on the collection plate.'

'Now calm down, Frederick,' said my wife when I came storming into the kitchen waving the *Monmouthshire Gazette*, 'otherwise I shall have to treat two patients in this house for high blood pressure, won't I, Mrs Cooper?' Our housekeeper nodded her head, and our two children looked at me in bewilderment.

'Read that,' I managed to say, through gritted teeth. I went out of the kitchen and back to my study where I sat in my armchair, still fuming with anger.

A few minutes later Eleanor came into the study. 'It would have helped if you had told me on what page you had found this world-shattering piece of information,' she said quietly. 'In any case, I had warned you what to expect. That man is going to be another Amos Perkins, your late departed and not lamented church-warden. He may not be on the Parochial Church Council but he will be a constant pain in the neck. If Dai Elbow wishes to raise money for the church in his own way, there's nothing wrong with that. All you have to do is write a crushing reply to the old Pharisee. That will get your anger off your chest and put him in his place at the same time. You are quite capable of doing that, my dear.'

That night I had a phone call from Dai Elbow. 'I'm ringing from the greyhound stadium, Vic,' he said excitedly. 'Your favourite greyhound, who licked you all over when you came to Abergelly, has just come in first at ten to one. What with the prize money and my bet, you've got thirty quid already with six months to go. That must have been a good blessing of the pound notes. That's her first big win. You'd better put some money on her next time.'

The next morning I wrote to the *Monmouthshire Gazette*. 'Dear Sir,' I began, 'Your correspondent in last night's edition of your newspaper condemns the parishioner who announced that he would use his greyhound to raise money for the badly needed funds of St Peter's Church, Abergelly. If he refers to St Matthew chapter 26, verses 14 to 30, he will find a parable where the lord gave to his servants money to look after and use to advantage while he was away for a long time, "every man according to his severable ability". The man who has the greyhound is using that ability to raise money for his church, not for himself. I have been informed already that after two days he has converted one pound into thirty pounds. Perhaps your correspondent might like to indicate in which way he could raise his giving to a level of that proportion.'

'Take that, Canon Morgan,' said Eleanor when she read my letter.

7

St Peter's Church Hall was now renovated completely. The unsightly damp-ridden walls had been replastered and freshly painted by volunteers under the watchful eye of Albert 'Basket' Matthews, the retired plasterer who had been given his nickname because of the size of his posterior. All the missing slates on the roof had been replaced, and the building was watertight for the first time in many years. Floorboards on the little stage had been removed, and the moth-eaten curtains had been consigned to the dustbin. A ladies' working party was engaged in making new drapes with material supplied free of charge by the Premier Clothing Company, a factory in Abergelly which employed a supervisor, Miss Edna Evans, who was a member of the Parochial Church Council. The scouts had been forbidden to use the hall for football practice, and the number of Sunday School members had risen considerably, with the newly decorated classrooms providing the attraction.

All was set for the inauguration of my second Gilbert and Sullivan Society, with such a splendid rehearsal room available plus the new piano supplied by my father-in-law. Already I had been in touch with the committee of the Abergelly Miners' Welfare Hall about the possibility of a production of *The Pirates of Penzance* in the late autumn. A meeting was called for the fourth Monday in January.

As the benevolent director in charge of the new company, I had decided the cast list already. Eleanor and I would play Mabel and Frederick, the two leads; Hugh Thomas, the Major General; Ivor Hodges, the Pirate King; Elizabeth Williams (his school secretary), Ruth the Pirates' maid of all work; and Gareth Morgan from St David's, the Sergeant of Police. Graham Webb was itching to get to work as musical director, and he had suggested that his star pupil, George Thomas, would make an admirable accompanist. In the announcements in church and in the parish magazine I had made it plain that no lady over the age of twenty-five would be considered for the chorus. This had caused some resentment amongst the more mature members of the church choir, but I was determined to insist on the age limit. I had seen too many productions of Gilbert and Sullivan where the daughters of the Major General were more like his aunts, and where the school girls in *The Mikado* were more like superannuated school teachers. Graham had promised that quite a few of his pupils were available, and all of Ivor Hodges' young lady bellringers were anxious to join. This left me with the problem of the male chorus.

A few men like Dai Elbow and Willie James had expressed interest, but two separate chorus parts for men were necessary, the band of pirates and the squad of police. It was here that Gareth Morgan stepped in to provide the answer. He was a member of the Abergelly Male Voice Choir and he said he would canvass them. It was with bated breath that I awaited the outcome of his missionary activity on the fourth Monday evening of January.

The first to arrive, carrying a copy of the *Pirates of Penzance*, was Willie James. I was at the piano with

Graham Webb, who had come to tea with us, after coming straight from school. The scoutmaster strutted up to us, 'Are the auditions for the leading parts being held tonight or on a separate night?' he enquired. 'I'm going to try for the Pirate King.'

It was with great difficulty that I kept a straight face. Graham retreated behind the piano and blew his nose. 'There aren't any auditions, Willie,' I said. 'I have already cast the parts. I'm afraid that this society is not going to be based on a committee with sub-committees. Pooh Bah is my other name and I shall be every committee rolled into a single person. It worked well in Pontywen and I am sure it will be the same in Abergelly. There aren't any committees in a professional production. That's the way it is going to be here.'

He stood, looking at me, open-mouthed and was about to speak when there was an invasion of young ladies.

'Hello, girls,' shouted Graham. 'Welcome to our Gilbert and Sullivan Society.' The senior pupils from the girls' school came crowding around the piano. Willie looked bewildered. That bewilderment increased with the next noisy incursion into the hall of the Gareth Morgan contingent of a dozen members of his fellow Male Voice Choirmen. The scoutmaster left my side and retreated to a seat, where he sat down, thumbing through the pages of his score. By the time Eleanor had arrived after putting the children to bed, all the seats in the hall were full, with every member of my cast list in attendance.

Our musical director had arranged the assembled singers in their various categories. Sopranos in the front of the left-hand side of the aisle, with the contraltos behind them and the tenors on the right, supported by the basses at the back. Hugh Thomas had brought his three female fellow paying guests from his 'digs', and Ivor Hodges brought four of his female bellringers. I was more than pleased that my ordinance about the age of the ladies in the chorus had been observed. It appeared that the average age of those present was under twenty-one.

My wife came up and whispered to me. 'Well done, Frederick. Now would you mind getting me a chair from the classroom? What's more, you haven't enough scores to go round, have you?'

It was true. There were forty copies piled on top of the piano, and there were at least fifty persons present. Young George Thomas was practising the opening chorus, 'Pour, O pour, the pirate sherry', as copies were being handed around.

'Would you mind sharing copies?' said the musical director. 'By next Monday, you will have one each. Is that right, Vicar?'

'Certainly,' I replied, carrying the chair for my soprano lead. 'May I say how encouraging it is to see what a splendid response there has been to my appeal for members of the Abergelly Church Gilbert and Sullivan Society. I look forward to next autumn when I hope we shall grace the stage in the Miners' Welfare Hall for our first production.'

This announcement about a show in the prestigious Welfare hall provided animated conversation, especially among the young ladies of the chorus. Since all the members of the Abergelly Male Voice Choir sang there every year for their celebrity concert, it was nothing out of the ordinary for them.

Once the excitement had died down, the musical director announced the way in which he would be conducting the rehearsals. 'First of all,' he asked, 'how many of you sight read?'

Half a dozen hands were raised. 'In that case,' he went on, 'I shall go through the different parts of a chorus, one line at a time.'

At this stage of the proceedings one of the Male Voice Choir contingent raised his hand. 'I don't suppose you've got the music for this opera in tonic sol fah. Our lot would be able to sing from that, quite easy, like. But as far as these birds on telephone wires are concerned, that's Double Dutch to us.'

When the laughter had died down, Graham said, 'I'm afraid there are not any copies in tonic sol fah. In any case, you'll soon become familiar with those birds.'

'Don't worry,' interjected a large individual sitting next to the speaker, 'Charlie's always been fascinated with the birds.' This caused an even louder outburst of merriment.

The musical director tapped the top of his music stand with his baton. 'Now then, settle down,' he ordered, 'let's get to work. We'll begin with the opening chorus for the men, then move on to the opening chorus for the girls, "Climbing over rocky mountains", and we'll finish off with two of the choruses for all parts from the finale. This means that there will be intervals when some of you have nothing to do. Please be quiet at those times, follow in your scores what the others are singing. In a few weeks' time we shall be holding separate rehearsals for the girls and the men. Until that time, please be patient. Now then men, listen to your parts played with one finger on the piano.'

At the end of the evening Graham professed himself to be well pleased with the first rehearsal. 'Some excellent voices in the basses. We could do with a few more tenors. That's always a headache. Sopranos are very good and once again a few more contraltos would be welcome. There you are, you can't have everything.'

'If I may say so,' I replied, 'there is no comparison between the kick-off here and the one we had in Pontywen. I feel very encouraged. As far as stage rehearsals are concerned, they seem a lively bunch of people. All in all, I shall sleep very soundly tonight. Another step forward in Abergelly.'

When we went back to the Vicarage, Eleanor seemed unusually subdued. 'What a start!' I enthused as we indulged in a nightcap of whisky in the sitting-room.

'You can say that again,' she replied. 'You have a really good society in the making, Frederick. So good, that after this production, I think I shall have to retire gracefully from my position as leading lady.'

I stared at her in disbelief. 'What on earth do you mean?' I said.

'When I came into the hall tonight and saw all those young girls with their fresh faces, I felt ancient. I am now well into my thirties, love. How on earth can you insist on an age limit of twenty-five for your female chorus when your leading lady has long since exceeded that landmark? Looking around at your female chorus tonight, I would say that their average age was about eighteen or nineteen. The longer the society goes on, the gap between me and them will become uncomfortably obvious.'

'In that case,' I replied, 'I shall have to drop out as well.'

'To be quite honest,' she said, 'I think that is what should happen. If you carry on as the young hero when you are no longer entitled to be regarded as such, and you play opposite some lovely heroine in her late teens, it will be just as ludicrous as the other way round.'

'Hugh Thomas!' I exclaimed.

'What about Hugh Thomas?' she asked.

'Well, he has quite a pleasant tenor voice which I am sure Graham Webb could develop. I could then take over the comic lead. I should enjoy that.'

'What about me?' she said quietly.

I stopped in my tracks. 'I know,' I replied, 'you could take over the job of director and producer. You are just as capable of doing that as I am.' By the time we went to bed, we had decided that *The Pirates of Penzance* would be our swansong as Gilbert and Sullivan romantic leads.

The next morning I had a telephone call from the Rural Dean. 'I wonder whether you could consider becoming the secretary for the Rural Deanery for that society which sends out missionaries to Central Africa, the – er – S, – er – C, you know the one?'

'The SCCA,' I replied.

'Yes, that's the one,' he said. 'I know you are, shall I say, up over your eyes in work in your parish but it will not take up much time. The Vicar of Llanfynydd was the representative in the Deanery until he died two months ago. He had been as such for over twenty years. So the organizer for South Wales has asked me if I know of someone much younger who could bring a lot more looking forwardness, and, shall I say, imaginingness to this position.'

'As you say,' I replied, 'I have a very busy parish to deal with and many challenges to face. Could you give me an idea of what would be involved in this secretaryship?'

'Oh!' he said. 'You will have to come to their meetings in the deanery once a year when, what shall I say, their photographs and things about their work overseas are shown. You will have to let all the clergy know when it is taking place and where the – er – hall or whatever it is will be. I think that's about it, in a nutshell.'

'If that is all it is, Mr Rural Dean, you can give them my name,' I replied.

'The organizer will be in touch with you,' he went on. 'He is not a clergyman. His name is Mr Cyril –' he paused. 'I think I had better spell it out to you: Freebotham. I don't know how to pronounce his name because he wrote to me, rather than telephoned. I think it is a bottom, come to think of it. If I remember rightly, the Archdeacon mentioned his name the other day. Thank you very much for your co-operativeness. How is Dr Secombe, by the way?'

'She is very well, thank you,' I said, 'and very busy in her practice in Brynfelin. So you can see, we don't have much time to ourselves, I am sorry to say.'

Five minutes later, there was another phone call which confirmed that my missionary organizer had a bottom at the end of his name. 'Freebotham here,' came the clipped tones of the professional. 'I gather from your Rural Dean that you are prepared to take on the position of deanery secretary for our organization. I wonder if I might come to see you in the next few days? I shall be in your vicinity on Thursday if that would be convenient to you, to discuss matters pertinent to your secretaryship.'

'I must say, Mr Freebotham,' I replied, 'you positively take my breath away. It is only a few minutes since I agreed to take on the responsibility.'

'Well, Vicar,' he said, 'it is a long time since we had someone as young as yourself to act on our behalf. As far as the deanery is concerned, our society has ceased to exist. The time has come when it is due for a new lease of life. Now then, morning or afternoon?'

'Would you hold on, please, while I consult my diary?' I paused for a while to give the impression that I had a multitude of engagements to consider as I looked at the closed book on my desk. 'How about 11.15 a.m.?'

'Wonderful,' he replied. 'I shall write confirming it.'

Since it was only two days away, I could not imagine why he wished to do so. The next morning, I received a typewritten letter which began 'My dear Secombe, I hope you do not mind the informal beginning to this letter. I feel it will establish a firm foundation for a close relationship in our dealings with each other.'

I mentioned my new appointment to Hugh Thomas in my study after we had said Matins. 'I've met Mr Freebotham,' he told me, 'when I was in my theological college. He's a fussy little man with a neatly trimmed moustache and horn-rimmed spectacles. I think he would be better employed selling insurance or something like that. All I can say is that his talk about his society left us stone cold. I wish you joy with him, Vicar.'

'Thank you very much, Hugh,' I replied. 'Now then, about another matter. How do you fancy playing the tenor lead in the next production after *Pirates*?'

He looked at me as if he thought I had lost my senses.

'You mean – er – play opposite – er?' he got no further.

'No!' I said promptly. 'You will play opposite one of the young ladies you met last Monday evening. My wife is retiring from her leading lady role and will take over the production. I shall be the comic. You have a good tenor voice and Graham Webb will help you in voice production, I'm sure.'

He was silent for a moment, examining the carpet. Then raising his head and looking me in the eyes, he replied. 'Well Vicar, if you think I can do it, I'll have a go. I've never thought of myself as another Mario Lanza but if it means that I shall have to make love to one of those "young ladies", as you described them, that is something worth contemplating. I draw the line at my fellow lodgers, by the way. They were only there for the beer, as it were. None of them could qualify as a leading soprano, I can assure you.'

'I know that,' I said. 'They come as members of the Hugh Thomas fan club. However, Graham says that one of his senior pupils in particular, Gaynor Evans, has an excellent soprano voice. He is hoping that in a couple of years' time she will get a place in the Royal College of Music.'

'Does she look as well as she can sing?' he enquired.

'She was that eye-catching blonde in the front row of the sopranos,' I replied. 'This is the reason why my wife has decided to call it a day next year. She has decided to bow out gracefully and let the young element come into their own.'

'Come off it, Vicar,' he said. 'She is still a very attractive lady.'

'The answer lies in that word "still" Hugh,' I replied. 'I am sure she will be very grateful for your compliment anyway.'

Promptly at 11.15 a.m. the Vicarage door bell rang to herald the entrance of Mr Cyril Freebotham, who had driven up the drive in his brand new Morris thousand estate car at about 11.10 a.m. I had seen the vehicle from my study window. Obviously he must have been counting the seconds on his wristwatch to ensure that the exact moment had come to stand on my doorstep. Hugh Thomas' description of him was accurate in every detail. Mr Freebotham had brought with him a large folder, and after offering a limp hand for shaking, sat down in the armchair in the study. Putting aside the folder on the table beside the chair, he proceeded to adjust the knife-edged creases in the trousers of his black pinstripe suit, apparently without injury to his fingers.

'Would you care for a cup of coffee, Mr Freebotham?' I asked.

'Freebotham, please,' he replied. 'Don't let us be formal, my dear Secombe. Yes, I should be most grateful for some coffee. Black, fairly strong, with just a dash of milk and a spoonful of sugar or two cubes if you have them.'

I went out to the kitchen where Mrs Cooper was engaged in telling a story to Elspeth while peeling potatoes. The tray decorated with a lace cloth and bearing two cups and saucers plus a milk jug and a plate of biscuits was on the table. 'Black, fairly strong, for our visitor, Mrs Cooper,' I said. 'I should put two small plates on the tray, as well. He's very fussy and I don't think he would like any crumbs dropping on his posh trousers.'

She laughed and my young daughter joined in. 'Is he funny, Daddy?' she asked.

'Very,' I replied.

'If I come in with you, would he make me laugh?'

'No, my love,' I said, 'he is only funny to grown ups, not little girls. I had better get back. Would you mind bringing the coffee when it's ready, Mrs Cooper?'

'Of course, Vicar,' our housekeeper put her hand over her mouth. 'I hope the coffee is all right for him. I wouldn't like him to get the wrong expression about your new housekeeper.'

'If he doesn't like it, it's just too bad,' I replied, and made my way quickly back to my study.

There I found the SCCA representative festooning my desk with stand-up photographs of tribal chiefs, witch doctors and mud-hut inhabitants. 'I hope you don't mind, my dear Secombe,' he said, 'but I thought I would give you some idea of the kind of people to whom we are taking the Gospel in Central Africa.'

My blood pressure shot up to danger level. 'I hope you don't mind, Mr Freebotham,' I managed to say with difficulty, 'but I would rather you addressed me as Vicar and allowed my desk to stay as it was until I returned. You have had to move letters and some written notes to erect your propaganda material. I find that very intrusive and unnecessary.'

The little man wilted under the onslaught. He removed his spectacles and looked at me, blinking as he did so. 'My apologies, Vicar,' he murmured. 'I'll move these photographs straightaway.' He produced his folder and shovelled the offending articles into it with a shaking hand.

'In any case,' I said in much more modulated tones, 'I need space to put down the tray of coffee when it arrives.' I began to feel somewhat ashamed of myself for my outburst.

As he replaced his spectacles, he apologized once more. 'I had no wish to offend you, Vicar, believe me. My trouble is that I have come from the commercial world into an entirely different sphere. It is one thing selling insurance and another selling the Gospel.'

I thought of Hugh Thomas' comment and wondered whether he had failed at his former employment as well.

'Mr Freebotham,' I said, 'as a man of the cloth I should have controlled my temper and it is my turn to apologize. Please sit down and let's begin all over again. I can tell you that I am not always as irascible as I appeared a few minutes ago. I have a parish with many problems confronting me, and I only took on the obligation presented to me by the Rural Dean because he told me that it would not involve any undue calls upon my time. If you can assure me that this is the case, then I shall be only too happy to assist you in this deanery.'

He looked at me over his glasses. 'Let me put it this way,' he replied. 'Whatever you can do within the limits of time that you have at your disposal will be much appreciated. For the past twenty years or so, nothing has been forthcoming from this neck of the wood. Your predecessor was secretary in name only.'

At this stage in our conversation, Mrs Cooper entered, after a discreet tap on the door. She was followed by Elspeth, who was hiding behind her skirts. After putting down the tray on my desk, she was about to make her exit when Mr Freebotham caught hold of my daughter's hand. 'And what is your name, my dear?' he enquired.

'Elspeth,' she lisped.

'And how old are you?'

'Three years and nine months,' came the reply.

'That's a clever girl to know that,' said Mr Freebotham.

'I can count up to a hundred,' she said.

'Well, don't try it now,' I told her. 'Mr Freebotham and I have a lot to talk about. You go and listen to the rest of Mrs Cooper's story.'

As she was going through the door, the little man said, 'I have a pretty little granddaughter who is just like you.'

'Do you make her laugh?' asked my daughter.

He looked bewildered. 'Sometimes, I suppose,' he replied.

'I think you had better go now, Elspeth,' I ordered. My tone of voice produced an immediate exit.

When we had finished our coffee, I was regaled by a description of the important Christian work done by his society, illustrated by the photographs which had earlier decorated my desk. 'Now then, Vicar,' he said, half an hour later, 'I suggest that we have an exhibition in the deanery some time in June. The question is where and when.'

'The first part of your question is easily answered,' I replied. 'Our church hall has been repaired and newly decorated. I should be only too pleased to host the event here in Abergelly.'

'Splendid, Vicar,' he enthused. 'How good to have it on your own patch. I have a couple of suggested dates in my diary.'

He delved into the inside of his jacket and extracted an impressive leather-bound diary. As he thumbed through the pages, he whistled *sotto voce* an undistinguishable tune. 'Ah, here we are. How about Saturday the 12th June or Saturday the 19th June?'

I opened my cheap desk diary, purchased at a January sale in WH Smith. 'On the twelfth, I have three weddings; on the nineteenth, just one wedding at 11 o'clock, and the Curate can take that. He will have been priested in May.'

'Done!' he pronounced and stood up with his hand out-stretched. There was a noticeable lack of limpness in the handshake this time, as if he wished to reassure me of his good intentions. As I saw him off, he said, 'I must step on it. I am due at Cardiff for a working lunch at one o'clock.' He did not specify the venue or the purpose. I suppose he thought it sounded much more impressive that way, as impressive as the spats he was wearing. Cyril Freebotham belonged to an era which had come to an abrupt end with the advent of World War Two.

No sooner had the SCCA representative's gleaming new estate car disappeared up the drive than it was replaced by Dai Elbow's rust-ridden vehicle, belching clouds of oily fumes from its exhaust. I was still standing on the doorstep, wondering whether I should have undertaken the extra responsibility of being the deanery representa-tive. As he closed the door of his car with a bang, causing a few flakes of rust to part company with the decaying metal, he boomed, 'Hello, Vic. That was a nice little car that just left. Mind, nearly had a collision with it. That bloke was going at a speed. Good job my tin lizzie crawls instead of races. Can I see you for a few minutes? Won't keep you long. I'm working two till ten today and I've got to get back for my dinner. The missus don't like to be kept waiting.'

'Come on in, Dai,' I said, 'pleasure to see you.'

Once we were both seated in my study he leant back in the armchair and launched into the reason for his visit. Extracting an envelope from his trouser pocket, he announced. 'Here's the first thirty pounds for your talent thing. I didn't know whether to wait until the six months was up or whether the church could do with it now.'

'That's very kind of you, Dai,' I replied, 'but the whole idea of the scheme is that you bring all your money to the special service in six months' time.'

'The point is, Vic, that she've gone lame since yesterday. It's the back leg. She've 'ad it before. The last time it took more than three months to 'eal. I've been worried whether that thirty pounds is all I'll be able to give. I was wondering if I asked the Vet for some special treatment, I'd be able to race 'er sooner rather than later, like. In that case I'd 'ave to pay in money out of the thirty pounds. So I've come to ask you wot you think I should do.'

'That's very honest of you, Dai,' I said. 'Since there is still nearly six months to go until you bring your offering to the talent service, it is up to you to decide what you think best. If I were you, I should take the dog to the vet. That way the poor animal will be relieved of her discomfort, even if she doesn't race again over the next six months. You will still have some money to bring to the altar.'

'Vic, you're a gem,' he replied. 'I'll do that. If you can say a few special prayers in church tomorrow when I take 'er to the vet, that'll be a great 'elp.'

He got up smartly, shook my hand and was back in his 'tin lizzie' in quick time. As he opened the door to get into the car, he shouted, 'Don't forget those prayers tomorrow.'

'I shan't,' I said. When he put his foot on the accelerator to rev up his engine, the exhaust rattled as if at any moment it might drop off. It did not and he left the Vicarage, leaving a trail of smoke behind him. Suddenly I was aware of a little figure at my side.

'Is that car on fire?' enquired my daughter.

'No, my love,' I replied, 'it's just like the train, except that the smoke comes out from the back instead of the top.'

'Auntie Cooper wants to know if you would like another cup of coffee,' lisped Elspeth.

'Tell her not to bother. I shall have some of the special coffee I've got in the bottle in the sitting room.'

8

'Good morning, Vicar. I hear you want someone to play the harmonium at St David's.' A petite, dark attractive young lady had rung the bell and appeared on the Vicarage doorstep.

'I do, indeed,' I said. 'Would you like to come inside?'

When we were seated in my study, she proceeded to give details about herself. 'My name is Jane Davies and I live in Glamorgan Terrace. I have just passed Grade 7 piano examination with honours, and I would be glad of the experience of playing the harmonium. Mr Gareth Morgan told me that there was no one to play for the service and that you had to sing unaccompanied. I am confirmed and used to worship at St James, Penyllyn before we moved to Brynfelin. To be honest, I haven't been to church since we came here. So I think that it's about time I started going again.'

'Well, Jane,' I replied, 'I shall be delighted to have you as our organist. I expect Mr Morgan has told you that we have a very small congregation at the moment, about a dozen at most. However, once the winter is over, we shall be visiting every house on the estate to find out how many church people live there, and I am hoping that this will make a big increase in our numbers. So you can start straightaway.' I went to a book shelf and produced a music copy of *Hymns Ancient and Modern*. 'If you can spare a few minutes,' I added, 'I'll give you the hymn numbers for tomorrow.'

'I'm in no hurry,' she replied. 'It's my day off. I work in the Council offices as a secretary. I've come down by bus and after I leave here, I shall be pottering around the town.'

'By the way,' I said, 'are you interested in Gilbert and Sullivan? We are just starting a church society production of *The Pirates of Penzance*.'

'So Mr Morgan said,' she replied. 'Yes, I'd love to join. I'm a contralto and I enjoy singing.'

By the time she left the Vicarage, Jane was equipped with the *A & M* music copy, the hymns for the service and a parish magazine, plus a score of *Pirates*.

After she had left, Eleanor came into the study with the two children. 'We are going out shopping,' she said. 'As it is such a nice morning, we may drive out into the country afterwards. Do you want to come?'

'I'd love to,' I replied, 'but I have two sermons to prepare for tomorrow. So I think I had better concentrate on that. If Mrs Cooper will babysit, perhaps we could go somewhere for a drink tonight.'

'Secombe!' she said sharply. 'You should get your priorities right. It is more important that you come out with your family, than arrange a booze-up later on. Why can't you prepare your sermons this evening? Saturday is the only day we have together.'

I was not prepared for this onslaught, which had caught me with my metaphorical chin unguarded. I looked at her in a daze. 'Well?' she demanded.

'What – er – can I say?' I murmured. 'I – er – suppose I can do my sermons tonight instead of this morning.'

'Right!' she said. 'I'll go and tell Mrs Cooper not to bother about lunch. We'll have it somewhere out in the country after we have been to the shops. If you can bide your time for a few minutes, I'll collect some cutlery and some paper plates plus the luncheon basket. Then you can keep the children occupied in the car, while I do the shopping.'

A few minutes later, we were away down the drive and into the High Street. 'Let's play I spy,' I suggested to my son and daughter, as we waited in the car.

'Elspeth is too little for that game,' said David. 'I can play it but she can't.'

'Yeth, I can,' lisped Elspeth.

'Well, let's see,' I replied. 'I'll go first. I spy with my little eye something beginning with b---,' nudging Elspeth and directing her attention to the council bus at the traffic lights.

'Buth,' she announced.

'That's not fair,' objected David. 'I saw you showing her where it was.'

'All right then, clever clogs,' I said. 'You choose the next one.' My son spent an eternity, surveying the scene. 'Hurry up,' I commented. 'I spy with my little eye, something beginning with – er ...' Another long silence followed. 'If you don't get a move on,' I said, 'your mother will be here and you won't be able to ask us.'

No sooner had I said this, than the car door opened and my wife handed me a carrier bag. 'Put that between your feet,' she ordered. 'Now then, let's be off.' Once she was in the driving seat, she put her foot on the accelerator and we were away.

For a February day, it was positively spring-like. Down in the sheltered valley where we had parked it was relatively warm in the strong sunshine. We decided to stay in the car to eat our lunch and to go for a walk afterwards. As we ate the ham sandwiches which Eleanor had prepared, on the bonnet of the car, followed by Welsh cakes from Thomson, the bakers, I told her about the volunteer organist for St David's who had offered her services as a contralto in the chorus for *Pirates*. 'Do you know what?' she said. 'I have an intuition that there will be a romance between her and Hugh Thomas. Once he is priested and in charge of St David's, she could become his right-hand woman. If she is as attractive as you say she is, then who knows what may happen.'

'At the moment,' I replied, 'he has two loves in any case, rugby and cricket. Her charms will have to be mighty powerful to compete with them.'

'Wait and see,' she said.

When we had eaten our sandwiches and cakes, washed down with the local brew of lemonade, we went for a gentle stroll of exploration, with David challenging Elspeth in an occasional race. 'Typical of the male,' remarked my wife, 'showing off his dominance over the female.'

'You must admit,' I replied, 'that the female puts up some spirited opposition, despite the odds against her.'

'She gets that from her mother,' snorted Eleanor.

I was about to reply, 'You can say that again', when our badinage was interrupted by the arrival of a large alsatian travelling at speed, which went past us and proceeded to bowl over David, who was some yards ahead. 'Herman, come here at once,' barked an aristocratic voice behind us.

By now Herman was licking the face of our prostrate son, who appeared to be bewildered rather than terrified like his sister. We turned around to see a tall tweeded figure wearing a deer-stalker hat and wielding a walking stick as a warning to his dog. Immediately the animal left off its cleansing operation and returned to its owner, with its tail between its legs.

The middle-aged gentleman, who sported a neat grey military moustache, ordered Herman to sit and was obeyed instantly. 'My apologies,' he said. 'I'm afraid that although he is very friendly he doesn't realize that he is such a big dog. I hope your little boy is not too shaken.'

David, who had joined us, looked up at him and shook his head. 'I like dogs,' he informed him, and with his typical bravado, added 'I'm never afraid of them.'

'I am,' announced Elspeth, 'especially big ones.'

'I expect all little girls are afraid of big dogs,' replied the man. 'I must apologize once more to you, Vicar, and your good lady, for the boisterous behaviour of Herman. By the way, my name is Challenor and I am on the Governing Body of the Church in Wales. I take it that you are a local parish priest.'

'Very much so,' I said. 'My name is Secombe and I am Vicar of Abergelly. This is my wife Eleanor and these are our two children, David and Elspeth.'

'How good to meet you,' he replied. 'I have read about you in the local paper. Mrs Secombe is a doctor, if I am not mistaken.'

'You are not mistaken, Mr Challenor,' said my wife. 'I am in general practice on the Brynfelin estate, where I am as much a pioneer as my husband is in his new church there.'

'I don't doubt that,' he replied. 'What a splendid combination you two make, one with a cure of souls and the other with a cure of bodies. All power to your elbows. Well, I must press on with Herman's afternoon exercise. Good day to you both.'

It was not long before the man and his dog were out of sight.

'You know who that is,' I said to Eleanor, 'he is Colonel Challenor, the High Sheriff. His wife died last year after a long illness. He lives at Crawley House, that mansion facing the entrance to this valley.'

'If I had known that I would have given him a Colonel instead of a Mister when I addressed him,' she remarked. 'In any case, he did not look like a man who would be offended by the omission. No pomposity there.'

'None at all,' I said. 'What is more, he earned his title during the last war. He has a DSO after his name. He won it at Arnhem. Joseph Owen, who is his Vicar, told me at the last Chapter meeting that he is an excellent church-warden, even to the extent of rolling up his sleeves on one occasion and stoking the church boiler when the verger was ill.'

'We could do with him at Abergelly,' commented Eleanor.

'Come off it!' I protested. 'We have two splendid men at St Peter's.'

'I know that perfectly well,' she said sharply. 'I am referring to his influence in the diocese, which neither of our two stalwarts possess.'

'They may not be colonels,' I replied, 'but I am more than satisfied with their capabilities, thank you.'

At this stage in the conversation our little daughter came running back to her mother, to inform her that she wished to go to the toilet. They both disappeared behind a hedge while David came to join me in a man-to-man chat about the dog which had laid him flat on the ground. 'Can we have a dog like that, Dad?' he enquired. 'You know, a real big one like Herman. He could guard the Vicarage from burglars and look after Elspeth.'

'Don't you want him to look after you?' I asked.

'Oh, I can look after myself and Elspeth can't, 'cos she's too small,' was the reply.

By the time we reached home after our expedition, Eleanor and I had acceded to his request that we should install a dog at the Vicarage, but not too big an animal in answer to a further request from our daughter. It would have to be an 'in between dog', as David defined it.

When Hugh Thomas came into the vestry for the eight o'clock celebration of Holy Communion his right eye was bloodshot and a multi-coloured bruise decorated his cheek bone just below it.

'Good game was it, Hugh?' I enquired.

'Sorry about the mess on my face, Vicar,' he murmured. 'They had a vicious wing forward. He should have been sent off but he was too clever. He did all his dirty work out of sight of the referee.'

'From what I can gather, Dai Elbow always perpetrated his crimes in full view,' I said, 'that's why he was banned for life. What is worrying me,' I went on, 'is that your handsome features have taken such a hammering just when you are about to meet the new organist at St David's for the first time.'

'What organist?' he asked.

'Miss Jane Davies, who lives in Brynfelin, has offered her services and will be playing at this morning's service,' I replied.

'That's odd,' he said. 'That was the name of the elderly spinster who kept the post office in our village and who used to be deputy organist at our church. She was a little old lady who found the organ stool much too high for her. That meant her little legs were left dangling and she could never use the pedals. In any case I suppose it would have been disastrous if she did reach them.'

'All I can tell you, Hugh,' I replied, 'is that this Jane Davies is no elderly spinster.'

It had become the routine on a Sunday morning for Hugh to come back to the Vicarage after the 8 o'clock service to join us at breakfast, and then to travel up to Brynfelin in my Ford. In the kitchen I had warned Eleanor not to say anything about the organist's age and appearance.

When we arrived at the church, Gareth Morgan had opened up, and from inside the church came the strains of a Bach Chorale emanating from the harmonium. 'That's not the Jane Davies I know,' commented Hugh. As we came down the aisle and he espied the organist, he said, 'That's certainly not the Jane Davies I knew.' When we reached her side she finished her playing and stood up to meet us. Injured face or not, it was obvious to me that Jane regarded Hugh's visage as highly attractive, and that Hugh had the same opinion about the organist's features. 'Jane,' I said, 'this is our Curate, Hugh Thomas.' They shook hands. Perhaps a more accurate description of their meeting would be that they held hands; looking into each other's eyes, in the process. There followed an embarrassed silence which I ended by saying, 'Come on Hugh, let's get a move on. The service is due to start in a few minutes' time.' Then I added, 'I hope the harmonium is not too much past its best for you, Jane.'

As the Curate went into the vestry, her eyes followed him and then with a blush she turned to me. 'No, Vicar, it's fine. I shall enjoy playing it.'

When Hugh preached his sermon to the congregation of ten people, his delivery was unusually hesitant. After the service was over, he apologized for his inability to gather his thoughts, blaming it on the knock he had received in the match. As we drove back to St Peter's, he asked me for Jane's address in Glamorgan Terrace. 'I'm afraid I don't know the number. You'll have to get that from Gareth Morgan,' I said. 'You can ask her for that next Sunday. Why do you want it urgently?'

'It's just that I thought she would be ideal to help me with the Young People's Guild I'm going to start,' he replied. 'So the sooner I get to work on that the better.'

'In that case, you can call in at Gareth's house tomorrow evening and get the information from him,' I said. 'What makes you think she would be ideal for youth work?'

'She seems to have all that is needed – young, intelligent and lots of charisma,' he enthused.

'You have only now set eyes on the girl,' I said.

'That was enough for me,' he replied. 'I knew it as soon as I saw her.'

Later that evening when Eleanor and I were relaxing in the sitting-room I referred to the conversation and their holding of hands. It was my first opportunity to talk about the romantic incident, since Mrs Cooper was at lunch with us. When she heard me repeat the words, 'I knew it as soon as I saw her', she exclaimed, 'How wonderful, love at first sight. Echoes of our first encounter in the surgery, except that Jane has achieved that via the harmonium, rather than via Hugh's posterior.'

This set in train a pleasurable indulgence in nostalgia, in which we agreed that the Almighty must have been involved in my dear old landlady's painting of the bath which anchored my bottom and involved a residue of skin being left on the fresh paint. Had the senior GP been on duty and not the junior assistant, our paths might never have crossed. 'Thank God for fresh paint!' said my wife.

'Amen!' I exclaimed loudly, and we decided to go to bed.

The next evening at the Gilbert and Sullivan rehearsal Eleanor and I consulted Dai Elbow during the tea break on how we should set about choosing a dog for the Vicarage. 'Wot you want, Vic,' he said, 'is a boxer. They're marvellous with the kids. They look fierce but they're as soft as – er – sugar, I mean butter. There's a vicar near 'ere who breeds them. 'E's the Reverend Owen, the Vicar of Cwmdeilo. I expect 'e'll let you 'ave one reasonable, as you're both in the same club, like.' Joseph Owen was not only prepared to let me 'have one reasonable'.

When I rang the next day – he offered me a bitch for nothing, on condition that he had 'the pick of the litter', as he put it. He said that when the dog was 'on heat', he would come and collect it to mate it with another pure breed.

'How will I know that?' I asked him.

'Your wife's a doctor, isn't she?' he replied. 'Anyway, you can pick her up any time today, if you like.'

There was great excitement at lunch when I announced that we were going to have a dog. 'He said we can have her today,' I told Eleanor.

'Hold on!' she replied. 'We shall have to get a dog basket, a lead for her, a bowl, biscuits, tins of food and all the rest of it. I think we had better do that before we go chasing up to Cwmdeilo.'

'Why not do everything this afternoon and then pick up David from school?' I replied.

'Oh yes! please, Mam,' urged David, as Mrs Cooper prepared to take him back for the afternoon session.

'You're as bad as the children,' my wife informed me, as we made our way to the pet shop in High Street. At four o'clock we were en route to Joseph Owen's Vicarage, with two overwrought offspring in the back of the car. 'If you sing "How much is that doggy in the window" once more,' my wife warned them, 'we'll turn the car around and go back to our house.' That ended the vocal rendition but not the noise of their chatter, which continued unabated until we reached Cwmdeilo.

There was a long drive leading to the Vicarage. It appeared to be freshly gravelled, and the lawns on either side were in immaculate condition. Joseph Owen came out to meet us once we had parked the car outside the front door. He was a tall burly man in his fifties, with a booming voice. An ex-chaplain, he was the kind of man who would have been at home in the officers' mess. He was in tweeds like his churchwarden, and was wearing a red polo-necked jumper. 'Welcome to the pearl of the Monmouthshire countryside!' he boomed. He never spoke. He always boomed. Eleanor winced as he gripped her hand, 'So these are the Secombe brood.' Our two children looked up at him in awe, as if he were a giant in a fairy story. 'Well, my dears,' he said to them, 'I hope you are going to look after Lulu. She's a very nervous little dog but she is a sweetie. You'll love her.'

We were taken around the back of the house to what was once a stable in Victorian times and was now a dogs' home. There were five young boxers there, rushing to greet him when he opened the door. The one on the fringe was Lulu. 'Here she is,' he announced. Anything less like a Lulu was the ugly six-month-old specimen, obviously the least attractive of his litter. 'An excellent pedigree, as you will see when I give you the Cruft's certificate. The Princess of Wimbone by the Duke of Dartmouth.' Eleanor looked at me and I had to resort to blowing my nose, as was my wont in such a situation.

I produced the lead and collar we had bought at 'Williams, the Pets' Parlour'. 'Put them on her,' he commanded in tones which must have echoed around the valley. We fell in love instantly. She may have had a jaw which seemed to protrude at least two inches beyond the rest of her face but she looked at me as if to say, 'You are my lord and master from now on.' Apparently Mrs Owen was in Newport at the hairdresser's, so we were not invited inside.

When I was introducing Lulu to the rest of the family, the breeder went indoors to pick up the precious certificate. 'Lulu!' exclaimed my wife. 'What a misnomer!'

'Beauty,' I replied, 'is only skin deep.'

'She's lovely,' said Elspeth.

'There you are! What did I tell you,' I informed Eleanor.

Once I had received the Cruft's seal of approval, we drove off, with our acquisition being smothered with affection in the back of the car. 'We'll have to take good care of her,' my wife remarked as we made our way home. 'She's the nearest thing we'll ever have with an aristocratic connection.'

'I don't know about that,' I replied. 'My grandmother used to tell us that she once met Florence Nightingale when she was out walking near her home in Shropshire.'

'My dear Frederick,' she retorted, 'that does not compare with a Princess who had an affair with a Duke and whose love child is in the back of our car. I think you will find when you examine the certificate that she has a name like the Countess of Carmarthen, or something like that. Lulu is just her pet name. You could not stand outside the door of the Vicarage and shout "Countess", when you were calling her to have her tin of dog food. Still, we can't complain. We have had her for nothing.'

Back home we examined the certificate, which gave our new pet's name as the Countess of Radnor. 'I told you she would be a Countess,' commented Eleanor. 'I just had the county wrong. In any case she is Welsh.'

Mrs Cooper was as wary of Lulu as Lulu was of our housekeeper. 'She looks very nasty to me,' she said when she saw her. 'I hope she will be all right with the children.'

'Have no fear about that,' I told her. 'Lulu may look vicious but she would run away from a mouse, apparently. Besides, she will be very useful for keeping away tramps. Once she appears on the doorstep and they see that face they will make a quick exit. She's going to be a good guard dog.'

Hugh Thomas made the same remark when he came to the Vicarage the next morning. He stood back a few paces as she appeared at my side. 'Where did you get her, Vicar?' he asked. 'I didn't know you needed a guard dog.'

'Come on in, Hugh.' As soon as he moved into the house, she made a bee line for the kitchen. 'You see what a fearsome animal she is, or should I say, fearful.'

When we were seated in the study, I told him about our visit to Cwmdeilo Vicarage to comply with our children's request for a dog. 'I must say,' I went on, 'as far as I was concerned it was love at first sight for both of us. I have a strong feeling that wherever I go, she will be there too. Now then, speaking of love at first sight, did you manage to contact Jane Davies last night?'

I had never seen my Curate blush. 'Come off it, Vicar,' he riposted, 'I went to see her simply because she is the only person on the estate whom I have seen so far who will be able to help me run the Youth Club I want to start. After our talk last night I found that she had been active in a youth guild in her previous parish. In her early twenties she is just the right age to be acceptable to the youngsters – someone I could leave in charge if I could not be present. Not only that but she is secretary to the Director of Education in the Council offices and that could be very useful if we applied for a grant to buy equipment. You know how short of funds we are in this parish. So, if you don't mind, I should be grateful if you would keep my personal life out of my parochial duties.'

By now there was a rising tide of anger in his voice. I realized that I had overstepped the bounds in what should be a professional relationship between the two of us.

'I must apologize for my stupidity, Hugh,' I said. 'I promise that it will not happen again. Now then, shall we get down to working out the list of parochial duties, as you put it.'

When he left the Vicarage an hour later we were on the best of terms. I never made the mistake again of intruding into his private life. It was a lesson I learnt for the rest of my ministry.

When David came home from school that afternoon with Mrs Cooper he wanted to know if he could take Lulu out for a walk in the park. 'Please, Dad,' he pleaded.

'You are much too young to do that,' I said firmly, 'but I tell you what, you can come with me and you can help me hold the lead.'

I was sorry the moment I said it. It was quite obvious that the dog resented his presence when he tried to hang on to the lead. Passers-by were highly amused by the sight of the Vicar bent in half in joint control of the dog with his five-year-old son, who was attempting to prise the lead from his father. After ten minutes of this tussle for power, I decided that the time had come to recover my dignity. 'Right, David,' I said firmly, 'let go of the lead and walk alongside Lulu instead.' This he did with bad grace and then sulked all the way back, lagging behind me with his head down. I was determined that this was the last walk in tandem with him holding the lead.

The next morning was the first Tuesday in the month, when I took my sick Communion Services. I left the car door open on the passenger side while I went into the study to collect my surplice and stole to put over the seat beside me. On my return I found Lulu, sitting upright on the seat, a picture of canine dignity, evidently intent on keeping me company. From then on, if I was travelling around the parish on my own, she became my front seat passenger, a familiar figure to the parishioners.

My first call that day was on old Mrs Greenway, a dear lady who was bedridden with osteo-arthritis. Her body was bent in half and her hands were clenched tight by the cruel disease. She was an exact replica of my grand-mother, who had been afflicted similarly. For years she was nursed in the front room of our council house by my mother, who had the occasional help of the district nurse. Mrs Greenway's spinster daughter, Alice, performed the same function as my mother, whose smile I could see mirrored in her face when she opened the door to me. She looked over my shoulder to see my newly acquired com-panion staring through the windscreen. Then she turned to me in bewilderment. 'Vicar, you've got a dog in your car.'

'I know,' I said, 'she joined us yesterday. She seems to think that she is a human being.'

After I had administered the sacrament to them both, dogs became the main topic of the conversation. The Greenways had always kept dogs, from Labradors to Yorkshire terriers, but never boxers. 'They say they are wonderful with children,' said Mrs Greenway, 'so you have got the best kind of dog for your family. I'd love to have a dog about the house but it's impossible as things are. It's enough for Alice to look after me, let alone a dog.

That's the only thing, Vicar, you will find having a dog is quite a tie. Having to take it for walks every day and then finding somebody to look after it when you go on holiday and so on.'

It was then that I realized that I had taken on something which might become a burden in the days ahead. In a busy parish, there would be occasions when I would be hard pushed to find time to exercise the dog. When I went back to the car, Lulu gave me one lick on the face and then resumed her regal pose. 'Don't think you can bribe me that way, young lady,' I said.

9

The following morning an ancient Daimler pulled up outside the Vicarage to take me to the Brynfelin estate for a
funeral. I had visited the relatives of the deceased a few
days previously. He was Henry Arthur Roberts, a retired
miner aged seventy, who had died of pneumoconiosis,
after years of suffering. Henry Arthur had left behind him
a widow and a large family of children and grandchildren,
none of whom had any connection with the church. When
we arrived at number 30 Evans Terrace, the hearse was
outside, together with a line of cars and interested spectators, all female and in a variety of garb, from pinafores to
shawls which enwrapped babies who had been pacified
with dummies in their mouths.

Mr Michael Donovan, the undertaker, came to meet me
when I emerged from the car. He was at the lower end of
the market in the Abergelly funeral services circle. 'Good
morning, Father,' he said. A practising Roman Catholic,
he always addressed Anglican clergy in this fashion, even
if they were so low church that they referred to the altar
as the holy table. 'I thought I had better warn you that
they have got one of those "holy Joes" in there,' he whispered in confidential tones. 'I think he's in charge of one
of those Pentecostal places further up the valley. It seems
he used to work with the deceased in the same
colliery. He would like to take part in the service.'

'With pleasure,' I replied. Half an hour later I regretted that I had used that phrase.

There was a large group of men on the path and the doorstep, enjoying a cigarette before being called inside for the last rites. Inside the front room, the female mourners were packed like sardines around the coffin, which stood on trestles supplied by Mr Donovan. Standing by the coffin was a little sallow-faced man, dressed in black and wearing a black tie. He was thumbing through the pages of a Bible, licking his fingers as he turned over each page. I went to shake hands with the widow, who was seated on one of the few chairs in the room. She was surrounded by a phalanx of her daughters and was dry-eyed.

As I held her hand, she said, 'I 'ope you don't mind, Vicar, but Mr David Evans would like to take part in the service. 'E used to work with my 'usband in the pit years ago.'

This was the signal for the little man to come forward with the Bible in one hand and the other hand outstretched. 'Good morning, Reverend,' he breathed. 'H'I am in charge of the Salem Pentecostal Church in Abergwynfi and I was a workmate of 'Arry for many years. If you could h'allow me to say a few prayers at the h'end of your service H'I would be very grateful.'

'By all means Mr Evans,' I replied, disengaging my digits from his sweaty grip.

When all the sons and sons-in-law had abandoned their cigarettes and crowded into the room and its doorway, I began my reading from the seventh chapter of the Book of Revelation. I recited the twenty-third psalm and read prayers from my devotional manual. Then I turned to

David Evans, who was straining at the leash to launch into his contribution.

As soon as I nodded to him, he raised his eyes to heaven and addressed the Almighty in a loud voice. 'Ho Lord, we are gathered together 'ere this morning to recommend into your 'ands 'Arry Roberts, a good man who never did anybody any 'arm in 'is 'ole life. I remember the first time I met 'im. We was just children starting underground in those days. 'E shared with me 'is bit of bread and cheese that day because I'd left mine behind at the top. That's the kind of man 'e was.'

This peroration continued for another ten minutes, by which time he had only reached the time of 'Arry's marriage.

It was at this stage in the proceedings that the undertaker pushed his way through the throng and coughed loudly. Apparently David was deaf. He showed no sign that he had heard the time signal. 'I remember the joy 'e felt when little Blodwen was born, and then not long after when William 'enry came along.' Michael Donovan could not contain himself any longer. He advanced upon the supplicant, who seemed to be unaware of any other presence in the room, except that of the Almighty. That illusion was shattered by a violent dig in the ribs by the undertaker.

'We're going to be late at the cemetery and I've got another funeral after this,' he hissed, in what was intended to be a stage whisper but was heard clearly by everybody, including those who were thronging the passage. There was universal relief when the 'prayer' was cut short in its prime. The bearers were summoned peremptorily to remove the coffin. That was followed by the allocation of the male mourners to each of the waiting cars. In no time at all the cortege was travelling at undignified speed towards Abergelly Public Cemetery.

Then it happened. Halfway down the hill, on the bend where the church hall piano had disappeared from the back of the coal lorry, the hearse came suddenly to a halt. A bumper-to-bumper collision of the following cars was avoided by the narrowest of margins. I was travelling in the front of the first car, whose bonnet was in close contact with the deceased.

'That's been going to happen for a long time,' commented my driver.

'What has?' I enquired.

'That hearse has had it. It was third- or fourth-hand when he bought it.'

By now clouds of steam were enveloping the opened bonnet of the hearse. The driver and the undertaker were out on the road looking helplessly at their machine.

'Excuse me,' said my driver, 'but I'll have to go and see what's what.' He was joined by some of the men from the back of the Daimler.

Soon there was a crowd of disgruntled mourners besieging the unfortunate Michael Donovan. I decided to stay in the car. I had no wish to add to his discomfort. All this time every vehicle going up the hill contained interested spectators as they passed the stricken convoy. The next minute the undertaker and the driver, plus our contingent of mourners, returned to the Daimler. Opening the car door, the embarrassed funeral director said to me, 'Sorry abut this – er – delay, Father. If you don't mind, I'll have to come into the front along with you. We'll take all the mourners down to the cemetery and they can wait in the chapel until we can bring the coffin. I'll phone up the Co-op as soon as we get down to the cemetery to see if they've got a spare hearse.'

As we sat in close proximity I became aware of the aroma of whisky, mingled with its disguise of peppermint and the smell of mothballs indicating the presence of the additional passenger. 'Holy Mary, Mother of God,' he exclaimed. 'Sorry, Father, but this could not have come at a worse moment. I've got another funeral at half past twelve and it's a quarter to twelve now. Suppose they haven't got a hearse at the Co-op. We'll have to get a van or something to bring the coffin I suppose, but I can't go to the next funeral with a van. I'll never live it down in Abergelly. Put your foot down on that accelerator, Charlie.'

Charlie gave his boss a hostile look and put his foot down, which caused his limousine to jerk forward. The undertaker's face, in concert with mine, linked up inches away from the windscreen. From the back of the car came a stream of loud obscenities from the mourners. 'There was no need for that, Charlie,' shouted Mr Donovan. An argument between the two ensued, in the course of which the driver informed his boss that it was time he put his hand in his pocket a bit more. When we entered the cemetery gates at a speed more appropriate to Brands Hatch than a burial ground, the cemetery superintendent emerged from his office, looking startled. The undertaker leaped from the Daimler as soon as it stopped, shutting the door with a loud bang.

'What's happening?' enquired the council official.

'The bloody hearse has broken down up on the Bryn-felin hill. Can I use your phone?' came the exasperated reply.

As the next two funeral coaches appeared, followed by three private cars, I thought the time had come for me to head off a riot amongst the mourners. First of all I had to deal with the sons and sons-in-law who were travelling in the Daimler. They were about to descend upon the recalcitrant driver as they scrambled out of the car. 'Gentlemen,' I said, 'let's calm down. The driver had orders to step on it to enable Mr Donovan to phone for help. Unfortunately his foot must have slipped on the accelerator.'

'You can say that again, Reverend,' exclaimed the eldest son. 'What a way to come to my father's funeral.'

By now we were joined by the other mourners. 'I am very sorry for this unfortunate situation,' I went on. 'You are all asked to come into the chapel and wait there for the hearse to arrive. The undertaker is trying to find another hearse. As soon as that happens then we can begin the service. Until then, all we can do is to have patience.'

It was a cold cloudy morning, and already there were spots of rain heralding the prospect of much more to come. 'The Reverend is right,' said the Pentecostal 'pastor', emerging from the scrum of discontents. 'Patience is wot we must 'ave, and of course, trust in the Lord who will put all things right.'

Suddenly there was a downpour of rain, which caused a stampede in the direction of the chapel. There was much puffing and blowing as everybody pushed into the bleak building. I heard someone say behind me, 'It's bad enough to 'ave the bloody rain without that 'oly Joe putting his oar in.' The smell of wet clothing mingled with the mustiness of the surroundings. Those wearing bowler hats shook off the drops of water surrounding the crown. Henry Arthur's send off had become a deeply depressing farewell. David Evans came up to me, 'Wot about singing a few hymns while we wait? I'll give out the books.'

'That's very kind of you, Mr Evans,' I replied, 'but I don't think the mourners are in the mood to sing hymns. No doubt Mr Donovan will come and give us news about another hearse any moment now.'

It was the cue for the undertaker's entrance. He appeared at the open door and informed us that the Co-op had not been able to supply us with a hearse, but that Harrison the Garage were sending their pick-up truck. 'If you will bear with me, gentlemen, the deceased will be with us in another quarter of an hour.' Whereupon he ran back to the cemetery office in a most undignified fashion, since the rain was coming down in stair rod fashion. As we listened to the heavens descending on the chapel roof with the intensity of machine gunfire, we all contemplated the drenching which confronted us.

'They didn't predict this on the wireless this morning,' said William Henry Roberts, eldest son of the deceased. 'We could 'ave brought umbrellas otherwise.'

Once again the Pentecostal man of God gave us consolation. 'Everything is in the Lord's 'ands,' he intoned. 'Maybe that when the time comes for our brother 'Arry to join us, the rain will have passed away.'

'Like 'Arry,' I thought, and repressed an unseemly urge to giggle. As the minutes went by, conversation began to develop about rugby, politics local and national, and the latest programme of 'Welsh Rarebit' on the wireless. To everybody's great relief the rough-sounding engine of the garage pick-up truck was heard outside, chugging its way to the chapel. The Lord must have heard David's words because the rain had ceased and there was an attempt by the sun to peep over the shoulders of the dark clouds which had emptied themselves upon Abergelly.

The mood amongst the mourners changed with the weather. They were ready to pay their last respects in a manner untroubled by the events of the last half hour. Michael Donovan came up to me and suggested that we omit any service in the chapel. 'I've got to be at Brynfelin again in a quarter of an hour, Father. God knows it's going to be bad enough to come with a truck to collect the coffin, let alone be half an hour late.'

It was a request I could not refuse. The mourners had already seen enough of that building in any case. The one request which I did refuse was from David Evans, who asked if he might add his 'few words' after the committal.

'The undertaker has to get away immediately for another funeral as you know, Mr Evans,' I said. 'I am sure the family are grateful for your words in the house, as it is.'

As I stood at the graveside reading the sentences from the Book of Common Prayer when the coffin was laid to rest, all the affront to the dignity of the occasion caused by the breakdown of the hearse was eradicated by the sheer comforting beauty of the words from the Authorized Version of the Bible and the Book of Common Prayer. Henry Arthur Roberts was delivered into the hands of the Almighty in the same way that Kings and Queens had been buried in past centuries. Before God there is no distinction of rank and class. It mattered not that his body had come from a council house and had to be transported on a truck. His final resting place was the good earth, the same good earth which has covered all humanity down through the ages.

'I hope you did not get caught in that dreadful downpour,' said Eleanor when she came home from her stint of house visiting. 'I got wet just going from the car to the house.'

'Owing to the supplication of David Evans, the man in charge of Salem Pentecostal Church somewhere up the valley, whilst we were closeted in the Cemetery Chapel the rain ceased just as we were about to go to the graveside.'

When I recounted the events of the morning, she said, 'From what I can gather the Irish gentleman seems to have a monopoly of the burials at Brynfelin, obviously from your account because he is so cheap and uses vehicles which should be on the scrap heap. However, it will only require a few more incidents like that of this morning and he will lose his custom rapidly.

'Now then,' she went on, 'I have some bad news for you, I'm afraid. Eddie Roberts' mother came in for an examination. It looks as if she has got breast cancer, though I may be wrong. Anyway, I have arranged for her to go to hospital for an X-ray. Let's hope my diagnosis is wrong. She is such a lovely lady, Eddie would be devastated.'

Eddie had become a stalwart at St David's, the one and only server and an indefatigable helper to Gareth Morgan, who was now acting as unofficial churchwarden. The young man had recovered completely from his accident. He showed signs of his injury with its permanent scars, but his limp had disappeared and he was talking about going back to work at the colliery. He was devoted to his mother, whose loving care had contributed so much to his recovery. To watch her die of cancer would be more cruel for him than it would be for her.

'Will it be fatal, if your diagnosis is correct?' I asked my wife.

'Not necessarily so,' she replied, 'it's only the one breast which seems to be affected. That could be removed by surgery and she could continue to live for many years as long as the cancer has not spread. Let's pray that is the case.'

'Amen,' I said fervently.

After lunch there was a ring at the doorbell, which had been heralded by the noisy entrance of Hugh Thomas' MG. My car was in Harrison's garage for a service. We were due to go to Cwmarfon for the deanery Chapter meeting, and the Curate was only too willing to offer me a lift. It gave him a chance to show off his ancient sports car, which could still reach eighty miles an hour, if given its head. 'Now then, Hugh,' I warned him as I squeezed into the passenger seat, 'drive carefully, please.'

'Of course, Vicar,' he replied unconvincingly.

As we moved out into the open road I watched the speedometer as it swung swiftly towards the sixty miles an hour mark. 'Would you mind taking your foot off the accelerator?' I asked. 'I have already suffered a traumatic experience in Donovan the undertaker's Daimler a few hours ago. We still have twenty minutes before the meeting starts and

I am not exactly eager to be at that dreadful example of modern utility architecture before time.'

Built at a low cost a few years previously, the Church Hall was designed to create claustrophobia with its low ceiling and its airless interior. Since it was the only 'modern' hall in the deanery, the Rural Dean had decided that this was the obvious venue for the post-war era. Its Vicar, the Reverend Geoffrey Thompson, who had ideas above his present lowly station, was hopeful that it would be a stepping stone to a place of honour in the diocese, perhaps a canonry and one day an archdeaconry. A bearded man in his late forties, he courted popularity assiduously.

It was Hugh's first experience of this quarterly clerical jamboree. As soon as we entered the hall, the Vicar of Cwmarfon swooped upon him. 'Welcome to the deanery,' he proclaimed as he shook his hand vigorously. Then producing a visiting card from his inside pocket he gave it to Hugh with a flourish. 'As Mae West says, come up and see me some time.'

Immediately he left us as he saw another cleric come into the hall. 'What a dreadful man!' remarked Hugh.

'Hear! Hear!' I said.

The next greeting to my Curate came from the Rural Dean. 'How nice to see you, young man. It's – er – shall I say – er – very necessary, indeed, essential to have younger blood to – er enliven the procedure.'

As the dignitary turned to somebody else a big hand grasped Hugh's shoulder. 'Not to mention the proceedings,' whispered Will Evans, Vicar of Llanybedw. Will had been my best clerical friend ever since my inaugural visit to the deanery chapter, and my Curate had met him on a few occasions at the Vicarage. Since Will had been a back-row forward at university and had played a few games of first-class rugby, they had much in common. We were joined by Ken Williams, Rector of Aberwaun, a neighbour of Will's. Together we formed a quartet and occupied the back row of tubular chairs, far enough from the front to enjoy the 'procedure' without catching the eye of the Rural Dean. As the chairman and the secretary conferred behind the tubular table, we indulged in some gossip about happenings in the deanery such as retirements, the occasional death or preferment, or even scandalous rumours which were much more engrossing.

Our talk was ended by a rap on the table. 'Will you all – er – stand,' said the Rural Dean.

We stood waiting patiently while he fumbled in his prayer book to find the appropriate page. 'Ah! here we are,' he announced. 'Let's pray.'

There followed the collect for Quinquagesima Sunday instead of that for Sexagesima, after which there was a search for the collect for the Nineteenth Sunday after Trinity. Since it was several pages away from Quinquagesima Sunday, it must have been a few minutes, punctuated by coughing and sighs, before we heard the beautiful words, 'O God, for as much as without thee we are not able to please thee – Mercifully grant that thy Holy Spirit may in all things direct and rule our hearts; through Jesus Christ our Lord.' As we sat down, Will Evans remarked, 'All I can say about that, is that it is worth waiting for, even if badly read.'

The Minutes were read by Tobias Thomas, the Chapter Clerk. Unlike Sid Thomas the secretary to the Abergelly

PCC, who read at a speed, which, like the peace of God, passed all understanding, Tobias made the most of his contribution in exaggerated business-like tones. The bulk of his weighty matter was an attempt to make a précis of the treatise by the Reverend Doctor James Woodward, on the provision of a new Prayer Book for the Church in Wales. As a précis it was a dismal failure. Since it took twenty minutes to read, there must have been few sentences which escaped his attention. In the airless atmosphere of the church hall, combined with the excess of electrical heating, his audience were comatose at its conclusion. Even the Rural Dean had to fight with his drowsiness before he could rise to ask if there were matters arising. Needless to say, there were none.

'Now then,' he said, blinking away his torpor, 'this afternoon the first item on the agenda is the – er – apportionizing, shall I say, of the – er – deanery quota for the next twelve months.' Those who were on the edge of sleep were suddenly awake as if summoned by a bugle call. 'I know that this is – er – the – er – shall I say, the actual decisiveness of the – er – conference to – er – sort out. Be that as it may be, as it were, I thought it might be just as well that – er – we as brothers in – er – shall I say, holy orders, could come to some – er – agreement before that – er – takes place. In this way, we can – er – go back to our flocks, as it were, and tell them that this is what we have – er – agreed.'

I had never seen such a transformation in a meeting. There was no one sitting. All were standing, even the Curates. The only two sitting were the Chapter Clerk and the Rural Dean, whose face had paled. There was Babel in the church hall, a confusion of tongues, a loud confusion of tongues. Slowly he rose to his feet and began to wave his arms. Will Evans, whose voice could be heard two parishes away, outshouted the rest of the clergy. 'Mr Rural Dean!' he bellowed. 'Can't you see what you have done? How can you expect us to indulge in a fix as fellow priests? This is a matter for clergy and laity. I know that there will be acrimony at the Conference next month. That is a part of democracy.'

By now everyone else had given way to Will. One by one they began to sit down, including the rest of the quartet in the back row. 'I demand that you take a vote on what you have proposed.'

It was now the turn of the Rural Dean to rise to his feet. 'There – er – is no need to take a vote. I – er – shall I say, will scrub off that item on the agenda. I know that whenever it – er – comes to the discussingness of money and what the parishes have to – er – pay to the diocesan purse strings, as it were, there is always a lot of bickeringness. I thought that we could – er – escape that by being – er – at one with each other as – er – those who have the shepherdingness of our flocks of people. However, so be it, as it were, I – er – make a bow to your – er – wishes. So that is that. Well now, the next item on the agenda is – er – another horse chestnut like the – er – quota, and that is where shall we – er – hold the archi – er – the archdeacon's visitation this year. Last year it was at – er – ...' He looked at the Minutes in front of him. '... at – er – Llanedwyn. Now then, are there any what you might call – er – volunteers?'

The silence was as complete as the vociferous protest of a few minutes ago. 'Always the same – er – what should I say – er – the same reciprocation every year.' There was a murmur of conversation as he consulted the Minutes.

Will Evans' elbow collided with my ribs. 'What's the betting you are going to get it?' he whispered. 'He's not going back over the next ten years or so. Your name will be in the forefront of his mind as the latest recruit in the deanery.'

The Rural Dean closed the book with a decisive flourish. He looked at me. 'It seems that Abergelly is next – er – in the – er – line. So then, Vicar, I shall be, as it were, grateful if you will allow your church to be – er – used for that deanery – er – annual, shall I say, examination.'

As we gathered outside the nineteen-fifties' monument to bad taste, breathing in the fresh air of freedom after our incarceration, Lulu's breeder came up to me. He looked entirely different in his clerical grey. 'How's that young lady doing with you?' he asked. 'Has she settled in with you?' I was standing by Will Evans, who gave me a quizzical look.

'It's all right, Will,' I said. 'Joe has provided me with a boxer bitch.'

'I should have known,' he said.

'All I can tell you,' I told Joe, 'is that she now occupies the passenger seat of my car whenever she gets the chance.'

'You are highly honoured,' he said. 'She spent most of her time with us hiding from every contact with human beings. By the way,' he went on, 'it's just as well that our dear Rural Dean dropped his first item from the agenda. Colonel Challenor would have been furious. He thinks we have been penalized unfairly with the amount we have to pay. He still talks about the way in which your little boy reacted to the assault upon his person by that massive hound of his. He was most impressed.'

'That's what he has inherited from his father,' I replied.

'From what I can gather,' he said, 'it's far more likely to come from the maternal side.'

While I had been in Will Evans' company, Hugh Thomas had been in close conversation with the Curate of Blaengwynfi who was to be priested at Trinity with him. 'Apparently he has had a boring time with his Vicar. He spends most of his time acting as a messenger boy, taking the dog out for a walk and running errands for his housekeeper. I suppose that's what comes out of being a lodger at the Vicarage.'

Father Archibald Rogers was an Anglo-Catholic, and his house resembled a pig-sty from what I remembered from my only visit there. As I squeezed into the front seat of his MG, I said, 'Well Hugh, I promise you will not be invited to be a guest at the Abergelly Savoy Hotel. My dear wife has enough to do looking after a very busy practice, and Mrs Cooper is fully occupied with looking after Elspeth and David. In any case, her cooking is not up to four-star cuisine when my wife is not available, which is only at weekends.'

'My dear Vicar,' he replied, 'I am more than satisfied with my present four-star accommodation. My dear landlady is an expert on cooking laverbread and sausage on Sundays, after her visits to Cardiff on Saturday cut-price excursions. What is much more important is the distance between myself and the Vicarage. Don't get me wrong, Vicar, but, as I told you some days ago, I prefer to have my private life completely separate from my professional occupation. I find that I can breathe freely that way.'

'As long as you are with me in Abergelly, Hugh,' I said, 'I promise that I shall not intrude upon your private life; on one condition, that is, that your private life does not intrude upon your "professional occupation" as you call it. If that should happen, I should have no hesitation in asking you to leave, believe me.'

He looked at me and then turned on the ignition. As the engine roared into action, he shouted above the noise, 'That won't happen, I can tell you.'

In no time at all we were back at the Vicarage where Eleanor was on the doorstep. 'The Bishop is on the phone,' she called out when the engine had ceased its uproar. 'We had quite a pleasant conversation,' she said, 'and his Lordship was just about to ring off when I heard the unmistakable sound of Hugh's MG.'

When I picked up the phone and announced my presence, my father in God replied in cordial terms 'Ah, Fred! I gather you have been at a deanery chapter meeting. How did it go?'

I refrained from giving him an accurate account of the proceedings. 'Oh, it was just the usual run of the mill meeting. The only thing of note, as far as I am concerned, was that the Rural Dean informed me that Abergelly is to be the venue for the next archidiaconal visitation.'

'I see,' said the Bishop. 'Well, I am afraid that you are going to be burdened with another responsibility. I would like you to be the preacher at your Curate's priesting at Trinity. You have been engaged in parochial work in this diocese for some years now. I thought it would be a welcome change to have a parish priest in the pulpit instead of an academic. Your words of wisdom, which come from the experience of what they call the grass roots nowadays, would be more pertinent than something from the cloistered confines of a college.'

I came out of the study and went into the kitchen where my wife was peeling the potatoes in the company of our two children. It was Mrs Cooper's day off.

'Well,' enquired Eleanor, 'and what did his holiness have to say?'

'He said that he has had a number of complaints about my ministry in Abergelly and that I am to be consigned to one of the outposts of the diocese.'

'Very funny, Secombe,' she said sharply. 'You would not be standing there with a grin on your face if that was the case. Come on, out with it.'

'I have been invited to preach at the ordination at Trinity,' I said, trying not to be smug.

'Don't put on that air of false modesty,' she said, 'and for heaven's sake write out your sermon this once, even if you don't read it. Nobody is infallible. Suppose your nerve gave way when you were in the pulpit and you stood there with your mouth wide open and devoid of words! Anyway, well done! I love you and I'm proud of you.'

10

'Have taken Elspeth out to the park. Mr Freebotham has phoned you. He says it's about something that's going to be held in the church hall about Africa. I told him that you will be in the Vicarage by five o'clock at the latest. Doctor Secombe phoned as well as Mr Freebotham.'

Mrs Cooper's note was on my desk when I came in from some afternoon visiting of the faithful. Ignoring the society's representative, I rang Eleanor. It was unusual for her to call me when she was on duty. Her secretary answered the phone, 'Dr Secombe has gone to her mother's, she says will you ring her there.'

A whole series of scenarios flashed through my mind. I dialled my in-laws' number in haste and was answered by a coal merchant. I told myself to calm down, and this time took care in getting the right numbers. There was an immediate reply before I could speak. 'Is that you, Fred?'

'Yes,' I said. 'What's happening?'

This time there was a long pause. I could hear her drawing deep breaths. 'I'm afraid, my love, it *has* happened.' She stifled a sob. 'Daddy has died of a heart attack. It was a massive thrombosis.'

Before she could say anything else, I interjected, 'Put the phone down, I'll be with you right away.'

I scribbled a note to Mrs Cooper, telling her what had

happened and asking her to give the children their dinner and get them to bed as soon as possible.

In no time at all, I was in my Ford and on my way to my in-laws' house, deep in the heart of the Monmouthshire countryside. As I drove up the drive to the mock-Tudor residence, my wife came rushing out to meet me. Before I could close the car door, she had thrown her arms around me. She began to sob uncontrollably. There was a deep relationship between Eleanor and her father. They both shared the same vocation and had the same pride in their calling. She still addressed him as 'Daddy' but her mother was always 'Mother'. This bereavement, sudden as it was, had caught her unprepared, and despite her professional background of detachment from the vicissitudes of life, had revealed her as a vulnerable human being who would take many years to come to terms with what had happened.

It was a while before the grief which racked her body had subsided. She went limp in my arms, like a rag doll. I stood motionless, not knowing what to say. My mother-in-law appeared on the doorstep. 'Aren't you two coming in?' she asked, as if I was paying a social call. There were one or two moments in my life when I wished I had not been a Christian. This occasion ranked with them. I had an almost irresistible urge to shout, 'Woman, what in God's name do you understand has happened? You have lost a wonderful husband, your daughter a loving father, and you talk as if I were just popping in for a chat!!' I bit my tongue, painful as it was.

'You must be terribly upset, like Eleanor,' I said. 'I was just trying to comfort her before we came in. I'll close the car door and then we'll be with you.'

A few minutes later we were inside the 'drawing-room', as my mother-in-law described it. Her husband referred to it as the 'front room'. Mrs Davies, daughter of a solicitor, had been brought up in a prestigious boarding school in Cardiff. Eleanor's father had worked in the mines before many hours at night school had gained him matriculation and then a scholarship, leading to a degree in medicine in the University of Wales. Eventually he moved into a practice in Pontywen, where Eleanor was born and bred. She went to the local Grammar School and won a scholarship to one of the teaching hospitals in London. By the time she had qualified as a general practitioner her parents had gone to the more pleasant and profitable environment of rural Monmouthshire. My mother-in-law had detested life in the mining valley. It was not long before she insinuated herself into the county set and persuaded her husband to take up shooting and fishing. He drew the line at hunting.

When Eleanor and I were married, she was disappointed at the match. An impecunious curate was not the catch she had envisaged for her daughter, especially since he came from a council estate in Swansea docklands. The wedding reception had been embarrassing for her and for my family. The two sides had never met since that day nine years ago. When we went into the house I wondered whether she would do all she could to avoid a 'reunion'.

As I sat alongside my wife, my arm around her, on the expensive settee, it became obvious that her mother was determined to limit the number of mourners. 'I think a private funeral at Pontypridd crematorium will be the best way to let him be laid to rest. A few of his doctor friends and their wives, a few from the Golf Club and their wives, and one or two from the Angling Club.' She spoke as if she were arranging a dinner party.

It was then that the rag doll alongside me came to life. 'Mother!' she exploded. 'It's my father we're burying, not someone from your social circle. He must be buried not cremated, he would wish to be buried here at Llangwyn. What about Willie, his brother in Abercynon, Auntie Elsie from Pontypool and all her children, not to mention Fred's Mum and Dad. What kind of funeral is this going to be? He was a lovely man, a dear man.'

She broke down into tears and again began to sob as if her heart was breaking.

'Pull yourself together, Eleanor,' demanded her mother. 'You are supposed to be the strong one. It looks as if I am to be the steady oak and you the weeping willow.'

My patience was exhausted. 'Mrs Davies!' I exclaimed. 'Your daughter is indeed the strong one. She happens to be a human being. Apparently you are a desiccated oak tree and consequently devoid of feeling. I hate to say this at such a time, but perhaps you don't realize that it is not some stranger who has died and is about to be buried. It is someone who has shared your bed and your table, by whom you have your child, who is heartbroken at his death. I am speaking not as a priest but as a man.'

She stared past me – she had a disconcerting habit of looking over your shoulder with her cold blue eyes when addressing you. 'That's just what I would have expected from you,' she snapped. 'You are a jumped-up nobody who thinks that because he has a dog collar around his neck, he has the right to criticize his betters. Let me tell you that I shall decide how this funeral is to take place, and when the undertaker comes this evening, he will be given details of what mourners are to be invited into his coaches and to the private service at the cemetery chapel.'

'Mrs Davies,' I said, 'he deserves more than that.'

Suddenly Eleanor stood up, her eyes red with crying. 'How dare you speak to my husband like that! Criticize his betters indeed. I tell you what, mother. You are his inferior, not his better. Come on, Fred, we'll go back in your car. I'm in no fit state to drive mine but I'll be back this evening to see the undertaker. As your daughter I have every right to a say in the funeral arrangements. It is my father who is being buried and his family must be present to pay their last respects. His brother and sister loved him dearly. I'll show you who is the stronger of us two, you'll see.'

We were out of the house and into my car, leaving my mother-in-law still seated in her 'drawing-room' before she had a chance to reply. It was a silent journey back to Abergelly, with my wife immersed in her own thoughts and I not daring to interrupt her contemplation. In half an hour we were back in the Vicarage. My accelerator pedal had never been pushed so hard in my determination to get away from the unpleasant scene of the bereavement as quickly as possible.

Once we were back at home I suggested that Eleanor should get a locum to take over the surgery for the next week or so. 'No, thank you, love,' she replied. 'I'll get somebody to fill in on the day of the funeral but that's all. I shall need my mind occupied otherwise I shall brood. I'm sure that Daddy would want me to carry on with my work. The first thing I shall do now, is to ring Auntie Elsie.

She can let Uncle Willie know since he hasn't a phone. You write a note to your Mam and Dad since they are in the same boat as Uncle Willie. Then I'll ring Josiah Evans, the undertaker, to put things straight about the funeral arrangements.'

From a 'weeping willow' to a 'sturdy oak' it was a most impressive transformation. She went into the study immediately to phone her aunt. I went into the kitchen where our housekeeper and the two children were having their meal. Lulu appeared from nowhere and assaulted my person in a violent greeting. 'Leave Daddy alone, naughty dog,' ordered Elspeth with her mouth full of food and spitting out most of it in the process.

'I didn't think you would be back so soon,' said Mrs Cooper. 'Will you and Dr Secombe be having a bite together? There's plenty of food in the fridge. I could do something in two shakes of a dead dog's tail.'

'No thanks,' I replied. 'My wife will be back out again before long, and I don't feel hungry in any case.'

'Lulu hasn't got a tail has she, Daddy?' remarked my daughter, who was developing into a chatterbox.

'No, she hasn't,' I said, 'and she isn't dead either, is she?'

'How can a dog shake its tail when it's dead?' enquired David.

'You'd better ask Auntie Cooper that,' I said, 'I've got to go into the study.' I went out quickly, closing the door before my faithful hound could follow me.

As I came into the study, Eleanor was ending her conversation with her aunt. 'I'll be in touch,' she said as she put the phone down. 'Well, that's done,' she went on.

'Poor Elsie was terribly upset. She said she'll be bringing my two cousins with her to the funeral, and that she's got the phone number of Uncle Willie's neighbour. So she'll be in touch with him straightaway. She said that she expects that all of his children will want to come with him and Auntie Florrie.' Since they had seven offspring and ten grandchildren that would mean a large contingent from Abercynon. Auntie Elsie was a widow like Mrs Cooper, and her two children were young ladies in their early twenties and unmarried as yet.

'Now then,' said my wife, 'Josiah Evans, here we come!' She dialled his number and waited a minute or two before there was an answer. In the meanwhile I sat alongside her at the desk and began to write a letter to my parents. 'Ah, Mr Evans,' began the conversation. 'This is Dr Eleanor Secombe. I am ringing you about my father's funeral.' There was a pause. 'I think you will find that there will be a change from the preliminary arrangements. For example, in the number of coaches required. Then, too, instead of a service in the cemetery chapel there will be a public service in his parish church. I shall be with my mother when you come later this evening. I thought I would forewarn you before you went any further with your arrangements.' There was another pause. 'I am so glad, Mr Evans, that you have done nothing so far. That means that we can finalize everything tonight. I'll see you then and thank you for your sympathy.'

She set the phone down and put her arm around my shoulders as I sat at the desk. She kissed my forehead and then said, 'Now you can carry on writing to your Mam and Dad. I'll be with you in a quarter of an hour. Then, if you will, you can drive me to Llangwyn and drop me there. I don't want you with me. You have had enough insults for one day. I'll tell you one thing. She won't dare to insult you ever again after I have finished with her.'

The drive back to my wife's parents' home was quite different from the silent journey to the Vicarage earlier on. She talked all the way there about the happy times she had enjoyed in her father's company, about his ability as a GP, and about the respect with which he was held, both by his patients and his fellow doctors. All this was to fortify herself for her imminent battle with her mother. As soon as we arrived outside the house, she was out of the car in a trice. I reversed the vehicle ready to make my way back to Abergelly. I looked in my driving mirror to see her waving as I drove away. I wondered what the outcome of the confrontation would be.

My father-in-law was not a churchgoer. He had been brought up as a Calvinistic Methodist, but after his entry into university to begin his medical training he became an agnostic. For the rest of his life, to his wife's annoyance, he shunned any attempt to induce him into organized religion. She was a member of the Church of England, confirmed at school and paying her respects to the Almighty at Christmas and Easter. Although she was a part of the Church in Wales, she always referred to herself as believing in the Church of England. Had her husband been confirmed, undoubtedly her visits to the parish church would have been more frequent, since it would have given her cachet with the county set which she courted so assiduously. He and I had discussed religion only once, not long after Eleanor had married me. Somewhat pompously I had quoted Lloyd George's comment on a fellow MP, that he had sat on the fence for so long that the iron had entered his soul. 'That,' I said, 'is the difference between an agnostic and an atheist. So take care lest by sitting on the fence for as long a time as you have been, your soul is mortally injured.'

'My dear Fred,' he replied, 'I have been on this fence since the time that you were born and so far, I have felt no ill effects. It may be that my soul has become so case-hardened by now that it will take more than iron to penetrate it. All I can say is that I feel so comfortable sitting there that I have no inclination to get off my perch.' His reply was so gentle that I was diminished in his presence. Never again did I venture to impose my beliefs upon such a man whose soul was in a much healthier state than mine.

When I came back to the Vicarage, Mrs Cooper was on her way downstairs after putting the children to bed. 'Elspeth is fast asleep,' she reported, 'and David is reading his comic. He's very forward for his age, isn't he? That Mr Freebotham rang again while you was out. He said he wanted to talk to you urgent. He said you can phone him any time up until ten o'clock.'

The man was becoming a very unwelcome thorn in my flesh. Although the missionary exhibition was still some months away, I had been bombarded with letters and telephone calls once a week on average.

I went into my study, found his number and rang him in high dudgeon. 'Freebotham here,' came the reply. Before he could say anything else, I launched into an all-out attack upon his unnecessary intrusion into my busy parochial ministry and my private life. 'Mr Freebotham!'

I exclaimed, 'I have just come back from taking my wife to see her mother after the sudden death of my father-in-law. I am so tired already of your incessant communications about your exhibition. Heaven knows how much more of this there will be before the great event arrives. I am very sorry but I am afraid that I must resign from my secretaryship. You must find somewhere else to locate your showpiece and someone else to be your deanery representative.'

I put the phone down and walked out of the room into the lounge, where I poured a generous helping of whisky and sprawled myself into the comfort of one of the big armchairs. Mrs Cooper came in and announced that she was going to her room for the rest of the evening. Soon after that I fell asleep. I was awakened by an ice-cold hand being pressed against my cheek. 'Wake up, Rip van Winkle,' demanded my wife. 'I thought you would be in a ferment of anxiety waiting to know what had happened between me and my mother.' She picked up the tumbler from the occasional table alongside me. 'That must have been some helping,' she commented.

'It was,' I mumbled. 'I'm sorry, love. Come on then, tell me. By the sound of you it must have been a one-sided contest in your favour.' She sat down in the armchair opposite.

'There is going to be a public service at Llangwyn Church prior to the interment, which will be in the churchyard rather than a cremation at Pontypridd. My father's side of the family and your parents will be invited back to the house after the funeral. You can pour me a whisky now, please. Not a tankard full but enough to cover the bottom of a tumbler.'

As I hauled myself up from my recumbent posture, I said, 'In other words, a complete capitulation.'

'Frederick,' she replied, 'it was not a contest, as you suggested. By the time I had returned, my mother had come to her senses and realized that she had gone too far in what she had said to you and in what she had planned for the funeral. I think she was shaken by our walk-out after her outburst. She is a snob of the worst kind, I know, but there are limits even to the worst kind of snobbery. Evidently in the loneliness in which we left her, she was confronted by an image of herself which she found most unacceptable. I hope she never loses sight of that image. Would you do me one more favour? Go on up to bed and leave me here to come to terms with what has happened. I'll be up later and will try not to disturb you, but by the look of you that will not be difficult.'

'Before I go,' I replied, 'I think there is one more reason for my sound sleep in the armchair. I have resigned as secretary of the SCCA and I have cancelled the use of the church hall for the exhibition. I have had enough of Mr Freebotham. I'll tell you more in the morning.'

She raised her tumbler. 'Here's to us,' she said, 'and more time together for our family.'

It was in the early hours of the morning that I became aware of Eleanor's presence in our bed. Her body was being convulsed by the quiet sobbing which had afflicted her as I held her in my arms outside the family home. I put my arm around her and drew her close to me. Eventually we both fell asleep until the alarm clock alerted us to another day.

Over breakfast I told my wife about Mr Cyril Freebotham's telephone calls while we were out and his insistence that I call him any time up until ten o'clock. 'I'm so glad you have finished with that gentleman,' she said. 'The Rural Dean should not have suggested your name in the first place. There are plenty of others in the deanery who have far less of a workload than you.' As she finished speaking, the telephone announced its presence in the study.

'The Rural Dean,' I forecast.

'I hope it is,' said Eleanor. 'You can give him the same treatment as Mr F.'

My prediction was right. 'Vicar,' spluttered the dignitary, 'I have just had a telephone call from Mr – er … you know, the organizing man from the Missionary Society. He is very annoyed at the insultingness you gave him last night when you told him that you were going to have nothing more to do with being the – er – secretary of this SSCA, whatever it is, and that he would have to do his exhibition somewhere else in the deanery. I can't understand this. I asked you if you would be willing to take on this – er – undertaking, shall I say, and you agreed to do it.'

'Before you go any further Mr Rural Dean,' I replied, 'let me remind you that I did so with very great reluctance because of the many commitments I have here in Abergelly. You told me that there would be little work involved. That was an understatement. I have been plagued by Mr Freebotham ever since. Last night was the last straw. My father-in-law died suddenly yesterday and I kept having notes left me by the housekeeper that Mr Freebotham had been ringing me constantly in my absence. I am afraid, Mr Rural Dean, that I cannot possibly do the job. If you had given me a true picture of what was involved, I would have said, "No" at the outset. I am sorry that he felt insulted. He still has plenty of time to find someone to be the deanery secretary and to find a suitable venue for his exhibition. I would suggest that you tell the next secretary to be prepared to give up a fair amount of time to work with Mr Freebotham.'

There was a long pause at the other end of the line. 'Well, well. I am afraid I did not realize that there was all this, shall I say, getting a lot of harassingness in being the secretary. I am sorry to hear about Dr Secombe's father dying so suddenly. It must have been quite a shock. Mr Freebotham should have told me about your – er – shall I say, loss, that is, of course if you told him.'

'I did indeed, Mr Rural Dean,' I replied. 'It is typical of the man that he is so single-minded that he neglected to tell you that. Anyway, I am glad to be relieved of the responsibility. It is more important that I give all my time and attention to this parish.'

'Quite so,' he said. 'Will you give my – er – very sincere rememberancing and heartfelt sympathizingness to your good lady?'

When I went back to the dining-room, Eleanor was clearing away the breakfast dishes before going to the surgery. 'The Rural Dean sends you his heartfelt sympa-thizingness,' I told her, 'and he did not know that there was so much harassingness in being the deanery secretary for Mr F.'

'Thank God that such an unnecessary millstone has been taken away from around your neck, my dear,' she replied. 'By the way, do you know the Vicar of Llangwyn? I expect he will be calling on my mother this morning.'

'Since he is in a different deanery, I know very little about him except that, like me, he is a recent appointment,' I said. 'Apparently he is an ex-army chaplain, a man in his late forties.'

Later that morning, I had a telephone call. 'James Johnson here, Vicar of Llangwyn. I have just been to see Mrs Thomas. So sorry about your bereavement. Your wife must be devastated.' Before I could reply, he went on, 'I wonder if you would like to take part in the service next Friday?' He spoke in the clipped manner of an army officer. His sermons must have sounded like an army bulletin in the barracks chapel.

'Thank you for the invitation,' I replied, 'and for your sympathy. Yes, my wife was greatly upset yesterday, but she is coming to terms with the situation. She is a very strong character. I think I had better wait until she comes in at lunchtime and find out what she would want me to do.'

'Quite right,' he said. 'Wait to hear from you.' I felt as if I should have saluted before I put the phone down.

What a contrast, I thought, between the two calls I had received that morning, the first from the meandering Rural Dean, with his distortion of the English language, and now from James Johnson, the master of précis. As my friend, the Reverend Will Evans, remarked as we sat at the back of the last chapter meeting, 'Look at this collection in front of us. What a motley crew, the ordained ministry. All I can say is that God moves in a mysterious way, his wonders to perform!'

My musings were ended by a ring on the door bell. Mrs Cooper, accompanied by Lulu, was at the door well ahead of me. As I came out of the study, a man had pushed past her and frightened the dog, which had made a bee-line for her basket in the kitchen. He wore a clerical collar which had come loose from its moorings. His hair was unkempt. His suit looked as if he had been sleeping under a hedge, and his footwear was a pair of tatty plimsoles, minus socks. 'Ah! Vicar,' he shouted, grasping my hand and pumping it up and down. My housekeeper looked as frightened as Lulu.

'Go into the kitchen, Mrs Cooper,' I said quietly. 'I'll close the door.'

I led my unexpected visitor into my study, and went to close the front door. He followed me, breathing down the back of my neck. It was very unnerving and unpleasant. His proximity was malodorous. Once inside the study, I steered him into an armchair. 'Now then, sit down, please!' I said very firmly.

The wild-eyed cleric appeared to be in his early thirties. It must have been several days since his face had been near a razor or a bar of soap. 'How is Abergelly?' he enquired in cultured tones. 'Settling in?'

I looked at him blankly, not knowing what my next step should be. I swallowed deeply. 'Before I answer that,' I said, trying to control the quaver in my voice, 'would you mind telling me who you are?'

'Now that is a big question,' once again shouting and raising his eyes to the ceiling. Then he whispered, 'I am still endeavouring to discover my identity. Am I a child of God, and an inheritor of the Kingdom of Heaven? Or,' this time *bel canto*, 'am I just a relative of the missing link, one of Darwin's Ape Men??' He reached a crescendo which could have been heard miles away, had we been outdoors.

I wondered whether I should phone the police. I decided to try once more to be in control of the situation. 'All I am asking for, Father, is your name and your parish.'

'You are the same as all the others,' he shouted at me as he stood up. 'You ignore the one and only question in life. Who are we?' So saying, he rushed out of the study and flung open the front door. He ran up the drive as if he were pursued by a wild beast.

I went back into the house. As I did so, Mrs Cooper's head appeared around the kitchen door. 'Has he gone, Vicar?' she asked. 'I could hear him shouting in the study. I wondered whether I should have gone for the police. Lulu is still shivering in her basket. It's a good thing Elspeth is asleep upstairs. She would have been putrified.'

'I am going to phone the police straight away,' I said. 'The poor man needs to be taken to a mental hospital.'

When I got in touch with the police station I told the sergeant in charge what had happened. He replied, 'Oh, that's the Reverend Phillips. He is in the mental hospital in Caeravon. Sometimes he gets out and he is away for days. He used to be the Curate of Pentyllyn here. The sad thing is that he is quite normal for a while and then he gets these brainstorms. Thank you for letting me know. We'll get our boys to pick him up.'

I put down the phone and consulted my copy of Crockford. Herbert John Phillips had a Cambridge degree, second-class honours history, and trained in theology at Westcott House. At that time he was Curate of Pentyllyn, as the police sergeant had told me. I rang Will Evans, to see if he knew the man. 'Oh!' he laughed, 'you have had a visit from poor old Herbert John. It's not funny, I suppose. Indeed it's very sad. Quite an able bloke, but always eccentric from his first days in the ministry. He would preach abstruse sermons which bewildered his congregation, not to mention his Vicar. Refused to do any visiting and became a recluse. In the end David Williams-Jones had to get rid of his Curate. Shortly after, he went into Caeravon Hospital. One or two chaps in the deanery have had the unexpected pleasure of his company. You won't have a repeat visit, I can assure you. By the way, sorry to hear about your father-in-law's sudden death. Our friend the Rural Dean told me about it this morning. It must have come as a great shock to Eleanor, but if I know her rightly, I am sure she will cope with it.'

When my wife came home for lunch, I told her first of all about the invitation from the Vicar of Langwyn to take part in her father's funeral service. 'I would much rather have you at my side, love,' she said. 'I'm positive Daddy would want you there rather than dressed up, away from me.'

'I told the Reverend James Johnson that I would consult you before giving him an answer,' I replied. 'He's a strange character, very much the Army Chaplain he was until recently. He sounds as if he preaches and says his prayers to orders. I had a much stranger man in the study this morning, the Reverend Herbert John Phillips. The poor soul is in Caeravon Mental Hospital. Apparently he breaks out from there occasionally. He pushed his way into the house when Mrs Cooper opened the door, and frightened the life out of her and Lulu, who has stayed in her basket ever since. Anyway, after a somewhat intimidating session in the study he dashed out through the door and into the distance.'

'What a couple of days these have been,' she said. 'Still, this morning I had some good news. The tumour on Mrs Roberts' breast is not malignant. If you had said to me at the beginning of this week, who was in the more imminent prospect of death, my father or Mrs Roberts, I would have had no hesitation in pointing the finger at Eddie's mother as a certainty.' She began to weep.

It was typical of Eleanor's mother that she had engaged a catering firm from Cardiff to provide the food for the post-funeral refreshments. My wife had offered her services to help with the preparations for the occasion but was informed that it was much more convenient to have the assistance of professionals at such a time. 'It saves a lot of bother,' said Mrs Davies. So we did not leave Abergelly for the service at Llangwyn Church until three quarters of an hour before it was due to take place. Since 'The Grange', Eleanor's parents' home, was only a few hundred yards from the parish church, there was no need of the limousines her mother had contemplated ordering before her daughter's intervention to prevent a 'private' ceremony at Pontypridd Crematorium, much to the chagrin of the undertaker. It had been decided that only one funeral coach was necessary to convey mother, daughter and son-in-law for the short distance to the church. Everybody else would meet at St Mark's.

Before we could press the door bell my mother-in-law opened the door to us. She was clad in stylish widow's weeds, with her white hair immaculately coiffured, obviously after a trip to Cardiff. She looked irate, rather than sorrowful. 'Did you see that dreadful vehicle just outside the gate? They all descended on me as if they had come for a picnic. You can say what you like, Eleanor, but your father would have expected a little more decorum than that for his last rites. I told them to take that bus, whatever it is, from outside my house. They did exactly that, just outside.'

My wife looked at her mother as if she were a stranger. 'Did you go to Uncle Willie and share your sorrow with him? Your husband's one and only brother. That is what Daddy would have expected from you. I am sorry, Mother, but what you have done is just another example of your inexcusable snobbery. Fred and I will make our own way down to the church. You can have the Daimler to yourself.' So saying, she caught hold of my arm and we walked in silence to the lych gate to await the arrival of the hearse.

There we found Eleanor's Uncle Willie and Auntie Florrie with their grown-up brood and their partners. She went straight to her uncle and put her arms around him. He was a bald-headed little man, whose face and head bore the blue scars of the mining profession. The two of them wept unrestrainedly, watched at a distance by the bowler-hatted owners of the Jaguars and the Rolls Royces. Eventually, when they had composed themselves, they were joined by my wife's Auntie Elsie, whose three-wheeled transport had just pulled up on the main road. This was the signal for another burst of emotion. Her husband, Amos Watkins, came up to me and asked where he should park his car. 'I can't put my Reliant Robin alongside that lot,' he whispered as he pointed to the line of prestige motoring.

'Why not drive into the "Monmouthshire Arms" car park further down the road?' I suggested.

His face lit up. 'Just the place, ready for a pint later on,' he said. 'I don't fancy going back to the house with that lot all there.'

By the time the hearse and Mrs Davies arrived quite a large number of the late Dr Davies' patients had made their way into the church. The Reverend James Johnson came down to the lych gate to lead the funeral procession into the church, his black scarf bearing the insignia of the Army's Chaplaincy department. Eleanor's arm tightened its grip on mine as her mother was escorted from the limousine by the undertaker. The bowler-hatted contingent had entered the church, leaving only the family mourners to witness the coffin being expertly transferred to the wooden bier.

The widow stood in splendid isolation. The Vicar came to greet her. 'The time has come for us to go to join her,' I said quietly to Eleanor.

'This is my daughter and her husband,' announced Mrs Davies frostily.

Then my wife went to her uncle and aunt and led them to the Vicar, introducing them as 'my father's brother and sister'. The next minute the funeral procession moved up the path to the church led by the ex-army padre, who barked the burial sentences in such a manner that they were robbed of their proper dignity. Inside the church there was a big contingent of those who had come to pay their last respects to a much loved family doctor. The organ was playing quietly, 'O, Rest in the Lord' from Mendelssohn's *Elijah*. We were commanded to sing 'Guide me, O, Thou Great Redeemer', my father-in-law's favourite hymn. This was the signal for a Cardiff Arms Park vocal contribution from Eleanor's cousins, who were arrayed in suits of varying colour, all of them with the distinguishing mark of a black armband. At the end of the service 'Abide With Me' received a similar treatment, to the obvious annoyance of the silent widow, who must have wished that she was in a 'private' funeral at Pontypridd Crematorium. We went out of the church into the spring sunshine. A robin was singing his accompaniment to our silent walk to the graveside, where the quartet of the undertaker's paid assistants performed their duties with military-like precision, in keeping with the parade-ground conduct of the last rites by the Reverend James Johnson. Were it not for the warmth of the singing from the deceased's family, it would have been a soulless ceremony.

As the widow inspected the wreaths accompanied by some of her bowler-hatted friends, the Davies family held a short meeting and decided to go back to the bus and then join Auntie Elsie and Uncle Amos in the 'Monmouthshire Arms'. After Eleanor and I had said goodbye to them, we walked slowly back to the house.

'I don't think I can go in there,' my wife remarked. 'With the waitresses buzzing around it will be more like the Beehive Café than my father's home.'

'For your father's sake I think you should,' I replied. 'Most of your father's friends will be there, and since some of them share your profession they will expect to see you, especially as you know a few of them.'

By now some of them were coming down the drive. A white-haired gentleman who was carrying his bowler hat in his hand approached my wife. 'My dear Eleanor,' he said, 'I haven't seen you since you were a sixth former in Pontywen Grammar School and you don't look a day older.' He pecked her on the cheek. 'Such a sad occasion and a terrible shock to you and your mother. The only consolation you have is that your father would rather have died in harness than being put out to grass like me.' Before she could reply he turned to me. 'So this is your husband. I have heard about your pioneering work in Abergelly as well as Eleanor's. You two have a lot on your plate. I would take my hat off to you if it were still on my head.'

She made an attempt at a smile. 'Thank you Dr Ellis,' she said. 'May I return the compliment by saying that you do not look any different, except of course for your peroxided hair.'

'That's not a chemical, young lady,' he retorted, 'that is the crowning glory of old age.'

My mother-in-law's Daimler had still not arrived by the time the drive was overflowing with the cream of the Llangwyn society. My wife mounted the doorsteps and invited them all to come in. Her father would have been proud of her. When her mother made her entrance a few minutes later she found that her daughter had stolen her thunder and was acting the hostess to the manor born. The widow was not well pleased.

When we drove home an hour or two later, the bus had left the 'Monmouthshire Arms' together with the Reliant Robin. 'I expect they have stopped for fish and chips in Pontypool,' said Eleanor. 'I wish I could have been with them. It would have been a much more satisfying meal than the triangular miniature sandwiches and the minute sausage rolls served up to us. Still, I have proved to my mother that I am not a weeping willow but that I have a heart of oak – in any case a much bigger heart than she has. I am so glad now that you persuaded me to stay. Otherwise I should have let my father down and that is the last thing I would have wished to do.' She pulled into a lay-by and put her arms around me. 'Let's have a quiet five minutes together,' she said, and we did.

Mrs Cooper came to meet me as soon as we were back at the Vicarage. 'The Archdeacon has just been on the phone,' she announced. 'I didn't know what to call him so I just said "your Reverence". Anyway, he told me to tell you that it's about the instigation next Monday and would you ring him when you came in. The children have been very good and they're just going to have their tea.' They both burst out of the kitchen and threw themselves upon their mother while I went into the study to contact 'his Reverence'.

'Archdeacon speaking,' came the intoned reply. I was about to say 'Fred Secombe here' but then decided to match his pomposity with a similarly intoned 'This is the Vicar of Abergelly'.

'About next Monday, Vicar,' he droned. 'As you know, the visitation is due to begin at half past seven, half past seven. I shall require a table to be placed in the chancel with three chairs, three, one behind the table, facing west-ward, and two on the other side of the table, facing east-ward, eastward. The two are for the churchwardens, as you know of course, when they come to present the church accounts. Apart from that I shall not need anything else. Did you have a good Easter? I expect you had a rise in the number of communicants now that you've a daughter church.'

'We had quite an increase at the parish church, Mr Archdeacon,' I replied, 'but I am afraid we had only twenty at St David's. In any case, that is double the size of our normal Sunday attendance. These are early days. I am sure that Easter next year will provide much better figures.'

'Very good, very good,' came the duplicated answer. At one time he spoke in triplicate. As Uncle Will said of the reduction of repetitions, 'he makes up for that with his quadruple Yes, Oh Yes, Yes, Yes!' He referred to the Archdeacon as 'Little Sir Echo'. I was looking forward to seeing the Reverend William Evans on Monday. I had not been in his company since the last Deanery Chapter meeting some months ago. I needed a good laugh after the tension of the last ten days.

On Sunday morning at the parish church after the Family Communion service Tom Beynon and Ivor Hodges came into the vestry as Willie James and David Llewellyn, a fellow sidesman, were counting the collection on the table. 'Any instructions for tomorrow?' enquired Tom. 'I expect he will need a table up in the chancel.' He had attended the Archdeacon's visitation for several years, whilst Ivor was about to experience the occasion for the first time.

'That was the one thing he mentioned when he rang me last Friday,' I replied. 'We could have used this big one in the vestry but it is too large to fit in the chancel now that we have had the choirstalls put there.'

The scoutmaster, who was more intent on listening to the conversation than counting the collection, put in a suggestion. 'Why not use one of the card tables from the church hall and cover it with a cloth?'

'Willie!' ordered Tom. 'Go back to counting the collection, there's a good chap.'

'I don't know,' said the headmaster. 'It's not such a bad idea. For card tables, they are a good size and that will allow a space on either side for venerable cleric to pass around it.'

Willie preened himself and took off his spectacles to clean them with a flourish of triumph. 'There you are, Mr Beynon,' said the diminutive Willie. 'I've always said you underestimate me.'

'One swallow doesn't make a summer,' retorted Tom.

'Apart from the request for a table,' I went on, 'the Archdeacon asked for nothing else. I shall take the Bible from the lectern in the pulpit so that he can place the sheets of his charge there after the Registrar has read the roll call.'

'Sounds like a school assembly,' remarked Ivor Hodges.

'The roll call is the only bit of the evening when you've got to keep awake,' said Tom. 'Most people go to sleep when he's reading his charge. He can't see that because he's glued to his sheets of paper.'

'Well,' said Ivor, 'after what you have said I can't profess to be anticipating tomorrow evening with pleasure.'

It was decided that we would place a card table in the chancel, covered with a cloth which I would bring from the Vicarage. I had asked the ladies of the church to decorate the chancel with flowers. Ivor had arranged that the bellringers would ring from seven to seven thirty, to impress the clergy and churchwardens from the deanery with the improved campanological skills at Abergelly.

When Hugh Thomas and I met for our Monday

morning parochial discussion, I could see that he was unusually nervous. The longer we talked this became more obvious. After we had finished our business and Mrs Cooper had brought in a tray of coffee and biscuits, he sat on the edge of his chair and, red-faced, proceeded to reveal the reason for his deviation from normality. 'Vicar,' he began, 'I think you should know that Jane and I are getting engaged. It may seem a bit precipitate but we are very much in love and want to settle down together as soon as possible. She is the first and one and only girl I have ever loved, and I feel sure that God has brought us together.'

'Before you say any more, Hugh,' I said, 'let me tell you that I had a curate once who said the same thing about a girl and then two years later married someone else. Without seeming too cynical may I suggest that now that the rugby season is over, romance may loom larger in your mind than it should.'

'Vicar!' he expostulated. 'I can't believe what a low opinion you have of me. This is nothing to do with rugby or cricket or any other sport. I love that girl. She is the best and most wonderful thing that has happened to me. Can't you see that? As far as I am concerned, I would have no hesitation in giving up rugby and everything else to devote myself to her and to my Lord and Master for the rest of my life. In a fortnight's time I shall be priested. That will be a landmark in my life. The next one will be the day of our marriage.'

'My dear Hugh,' I replied, 'I can see that you are deeply in love but I would advise you not to rush into holy matrimony. I had been ordained for nearly four years before I married Eleanor. You are still a deacon. What do your parents say about the engagement?'

His face reddened. 'They don't know about it yet. I only proposed to Jane last night. I thought it right to let you know first in case I should have to move to somewhere else since I would be marrying a girl who lives in the same parish.'

'In answer to that,' I said, 'I could not ask you to move because I married someone from my parish and stayed there. Janet is a delightful young lady and old enough to know her own mind. However, getting married is a costly business. You will have to find somewhere to live and furnish it. With your stipend that will be a tough proposition. I don't expect Jane's salary as a secretary in the council offices is exactly princely. You are still on cloud nine after being accepted by your beloved last night. Once you have come down to earth and reality stares you in the face, you will find that settling down as soon as possible means not months but years. I am very happy for you both, believe me. You have all the makings of an excellent parish priest, Hugh. You said earlier on that you wanted to devote yourself to Janet and your Lord and Master for the rest of your life. I think you should change the order of your devotion. At your ordination you will solemnly pledge yourself to the service of your Lord unreservedly. If you do that, your relationship with Janet will fall into line.'

He sat silent for a while, then he stood up. 'Thank you, Vicar,' he replied. 'I needed that. I tend to be a bit impetuous, as you know, and your words of wisdom are helping to put things in perspective. I am going to see my parents tomorrow. Janet is telling her parents this evening when she comes home from work. Between you and them we should have a good idea of where we stand as an engaged couple.' As I saw him off on the Vicarage step, he said, 'If Jane and I are as good a team as you and Dr Secombe, I shall be a very happy man.' Seconds later he was in the driving seat of his antique MG, and was roaring his way up the Vicarage drive in a cloud of blue smoke from the exhaust.

'I told you what would happen, even before he met her,' said Eleanor smugly when I told her the news, 'but I must admit I did not think it would be so frenetic in its coming.'

We had an early evening meal as a prelude to the visitation. 'What kind of cloth do you want to cover the card table?' asked my wife. 'I suppose you realize that if you have it draped to the floor on all sides, as soon as his venerableness gets his legs under the table he will get into a tangle with the cloth. In any case, I think it is far too small a surface to spread out the accounts. Is there any canonical reason why the churchwardens cannot come into the vestry? Why does he have to sit at a table in the middle of the chancel? Take it from me, if you are going to resort to a card table for the purpose you will be in trouble.'

It was then that I had a brainwave. 'Why not,' I said, 'bring the table from the vestry and place it at right angles to the sanctuary and have the Archdeacon and the Wardens facing the North and South?'

'Tell me,' replied Eleanor, 'was part of your training at theological college the use of the compass? Yes, it seems to me the only solution of the table problem, that is, if the Archdeacon is agreeable to such a radical departure from tradition. I still think it is ridiculous to have to use the chancel when every church has a vestry.'

'I think you had better have a word about that with Daniel Fitzgerald LLB, Diocesan Registrar, when he arrives shortly,' I said. The elderly solicitor had been a friend of ours from the time of that incident just after our engagement, when Eleanor had saved him from choking on a chicken bone which had lodged in his throat in a restaurant where we had gone to celebrate. Ever since he had sent her flowers every Christmas. 'The registrar has to read out a roll call of all clergy and lay readers before the Archdeacon delivers his charge,' I explained. 'He will do that from the Vicar's stall and then his reverence will pop up into the pulpit and proceed to bore everybody.'

No sooner had I said this than there was a ring at the door bell. It was Daniel Fitzgerald, with a bouquet in one hand and a suitcase in the other. The old gentleman was sporting a multi-coloured bow tie, a regular feature of his appearance. 'Is the lady of the house at home?' he enquired.

'She is indeed,' I said, 'and she will be delighted to see you.' As he came into the hall I shouted, 'Eleanor! Someone to see you.' She came out of the dining-room and was immediately presented with a bunch of carnations.

'Christmas has come early this year,' announced the Registrar. 'I felt I could not possibly come to Abergelly without bringing a small token of my regard for the lady to whom I shall be indebted for the rest of what remains of my life.'

'Mr Fitzgerald, you shouldn't,' she said with a wide smile, 'but I am so glad you did. Thank you so much.

Would you care to come into the sitting-room and have a small drink before you begin your diocesan duties?'

'Just a small whisky, if you have one,' he replied. 'I always carry a supply of peppermints to camouflage any indulgence prior to a professional engagement.'

When we were seated, Eleanor asked him, 'Why on earth does the Archdeacon require a table to be planted in the chancel in order to inspect the church accounts brought to him by the churchwardens? Surely the vestry would be the place to do that?'

'Tradition, my dear lady, and this Archdeacon is a stickler for tradition,' replied the Registrar. 'By the way,' he went on, looking at me with a twinkle in his eye, 'You will have to be prepared for one of the most boring charges. I have been present at two already, and I should say that at least half of his audience, or is it congregation, have been in the Land of Nod by the time he has finished.'

'Thank you for the warning,' I said. 'Now, if you will excuse me I shall have to leave you in the company of my wife while I go and prepare the chancel for the big occasion.'

'My dear Vicar,' he replied, 'I can assure you that she is in good hands in legal custody.'

As I came up the church path to the vestry door I met Tom Beynon, who was carrying a card table. 'Have you brought the cloth, Vicar?' he asked.

'I'm afraid not,' I said.

He looked at me in astonishment. 'You are not going to leave this with nothing to cover it. They'll think we're going to have a whist drive not a visitation if you leave it as it is.'

'I've had a change of mind,' I went on. 'I've decided to bring out the table from the vestry and place it at right angles to the sanctuary. That way it will fit the bill. The card table will be much too small on second thoughts. So you can dump it in the vestry and we'll carry the more substantial one into the chancel as soon as we get in.'

'I don't think the Archdeacon will like being side on instead of facing everybody,' said Tom.

'I'm afraid it's Hobson's Choice,' I replied.

The church bells began to ring out as we struggled to carry the heavy table into the chancel, watched by a few early arrivals, one of whom was Uncle Will. He came up to me as we were getting the chairs into place. 'Watch it, boyo,' he warned. 'The Archdeacon is not worth a hernia. In any case, what is the idea of showing him in profile? He's bad enough to look at full face. Sideways will expose his receding chin and that dreadful long straggly hair on the back of his neck.'

'This,' I retorted, 'is the only table in the church, apart from the credence table in the sanctuary, which would be far too small.'

'Well,' he said, 'this visitation will certainly be different. By the way, I like the sound of your bells, very impressive.'

'Most of the ringers,' I told him proudly, 'are young ladies.'

'Now that,' he remarked, 'is even more impressive. Do we get a chance to see them at a curtain call?'

'The only curtain call you are going to get is arriving now,' I whispered, 'and he is scowling already.'

The Archdeacon was making his gaitered way down the nave, carrying a large leather suitcase. Will Evans beat a rapid retreat from the chancel. His reverence came up the steps and stood surveying the arrangement for his scrutiny of the churchwardens' accounts. 'My dear Vicar,' he intoned, 'you must have misunderstood my instructions. That table must be facing the west end of the church not north and south as you have placed it.'

'I am afraid, Mr Archdeacon, that there is not enough room in the chancel for the table to be in that position,' I said. 'The only alternative is to have a card table but that seems to be too small and undignified for the purpose. I could cover it with a cloth to hide its legs, if you wish.'

'Better a card table than the ludicrous arrangement which you have at the moment, Vicar,' he snorted, 'and yes, a cloth to cover it. Yes, a cloth is a good idea, a good idea.'

Out of the corner of my eye I could see Will Evans sitting in the front pew in the nave, flanked by his churchwardens and apparently doubled up with mirth. I went into the vestry and asked Tom Beynon to assist me with the removal of the object of the Archdeacon's disapproval. 'I told you he wouldn't like it,' said the churchwarden, 'so Mr Hobson's choice was the wrong one.'

'Thank you, Tom,' I replied sharply. 'Let's leave Hobson out of it, if you don't mind.'

When we came out, Will Evans had arrived on the scene to help with carrying the table back to its home in the vestry. 'You are too little to be involved in this,' he ordered. 'You stand aside and let a big man help your warden to get it out of the way.'

In the meantime the Archdeacon was up in the pulpit, unloading sheets of paper on the lectern. I could see why the Registrar had said that the 'charge' had gone on for so long that half his listeners had fallen asleep. While Uncle Will and Tom were engaged in their transport of the table, I made a quick exit to the Vicarage to find a cloth to disguise the card table.

When I dashed into the sitting-room, Daniel Fitzgerald was on his feet and preparing to proceed to his ecclesiastical duties.

'Now then. What has happened?' enquired Eleanor.

'Believe it or not,' I replied, 'his holy highness has insisted that he wants to use the card table and that he will require a cloth to mask its identity. If you had not suggested that it would be unsuitable, we would not have had this hullabaloo.'

'Now, now children,' said the Registrar, 'don't fall out over the Archdeacon, it is not worth it. I shall go and calm him down while you find a suitable cloth.' He left the room leaving a strong smell of peppermints behind him.

My wife stormed off in high dudgeon to find a cloth. She returned a few minutes later with a large beige tablecloth. 'Here you are,' she snapped. 'It's large enough to cover four card tables. I hope he gets caught up in it good and proper.'

When I returned to the church, almost all of the clergy and churchwardens had arrived, and the bellringers were coming to the end of their peal. Standing in the middle of the chancel was the card table, naked, and the focal point of discussion amongst the viewers in the nave as to its purpose. The Archdeacon was still in the pulpit, playing with the pages of his charge. Tom Beynon stared at the cloth. 'Vicar!' he exclaimed, 'that is going to drown the card table, not to mention the Archdeacon and the church-wardens.'

'Well, here it is,' I replied, 'and we shall have to arrange it as best we can.'

When we unfolded the tablecloth, it became obvious that at least nine-tenths of it was superfluous.

'Hasn't Dr Secombe got a smaller one than this?' enquired Tom.

'I am not going back to the Vicarage again,' I said testily. By now we had a fascinated audience except for the Archdeacon, who was finding his charge most engrossing, and Daniel Fitzgerald sitting in my stall with his head bent over the list of names he had to call in a few minutes' time. 'Perhaps if we folded it in half that would help to solve the problem,' I suggested.

'Excuse me, Vicar,' said Tom, who was now exasperated, 'apart from cutting it up I can't see what we can do.'

'I tell you what,' I replied. 'There's only one thing left for us to do and that is to cover up the table, and whatever is left over, roll the sides into four neat folds. The chairs can then be placed on top of the cloth to cover up the table which is underneath them.'

By the time this operation was over the Archdeacon had finished his perusal of the charge and was on his way to robe in the vestry. As he attempted to pass the table, he caught his foot in the west fold of the Vicarage tablecloth, and landed between the east and west folds, pulling the table on top of him. It must have been the only time in his life that he had given such a *tour de force* of comic entertainment to an assembly of clergy and laity. The mirth in the nave was unrestrained. When he rose to his feet, his dignity in tatters, he announced angrily that the church-wardens must bring their accounts to the vestry. 'To the vestry,' he repeated in a rising scale of volume. Then he turned to me, red-faced and breathing fire. 'Vicar! Would you please remove this mess from the chancel before we begin the proceedings,' he bellowed. Tom Beynon and Ivor Hodges came quickly to my assistance. We dumped the tablecloth in the choir stall and deposited the card table inside the sanctuary.

All the time I was trying to control my unseemly urge to giggle, the suppressed amusement manifesting itself in an occasional snort.

The rest of the evening dragged on in anticlimax. As he left the church, the Archdeacon told me that this would be the last visitation ever to be held in Abergelly. 'Never again!' he repeated in triplicate.

'So much for my attempt to impress,' I said to Eleanor, after describing what had happened. Her only reaction was to collapse in paroxysms of laughter. Eventually she said, 'You certainly made an impression, my dear, and his pompous reverence has the bruises to prove it, I expect. It was about time that he had his come-uppance or in this case down-uppance. I hoped the large tablecloth would contribute to the evening's entertainment.'

The next morning I had a call from Uncle Will. 'Thank you for putting on the best piece of slapstick comedy I have seen for years,' he said. 'I don't think the Archdeacon will ever live it down. However, my dear boy, I am not ringing about that but about a letter I have received this morning from a William James, the scoutmaster of the scoop of trouts if you will pardon the spoonerism, in your parish. He is pitching camp in Llanybedw woods in three weeks' time and would like to bring the boys to morning service in our church. I don't suppose it will be possible for you to come and join us for the occasion?'

'Thank you for the invitation, Will,' I replied, 'which I gladly accept, or should I say, accept gladly. My Curate is being priested in a fortnight's time and will be able to celebrate at our Family Communion. I think he will enjoy being in full charge. By the way, there is a pleasure in store for you when you meet our scoutmaster. Willie is just the wrong side of five feet, is possessed of a Paul Robeson voice off-key, and wears jam-jar spectacles. He is a char-acter *par excellence*. I think you will find that the troop is in charge of Willie rather than the other way round. Do you want me to preach?'

'Of course, boyo! Why do you think I invited you? It's an opportunity to take the weight off my feet, if not off my mind as well. You see, I'm not blessed with a curate like you. To quote Paul Robeson (he began to sing) "If you can help somebody".'

'All I can say, Will,' I retorted, 'is that while you do not share Willie's stature you certainly share his vocal ability.'

'Why do you haul, to wrap things up. Why don't you say, "Your voice is as bad as his, if not worse"?' he replied. 'And on that harmonious note I bid you farewell until three weeks' time.'

That evening we had our first stage rehearsal for *The Pirates of Penzance*. It involved the opening chorus for the men and that for the girls. There was the usual excitement as the chairs were pushed to the side of the hall and I chalked on the floor the dimensions of the stage at the Welfare Hall. It was the first time, for almost all of the society, that they had been required to act. Just as at the similar occasion in Pontywen, the men recovered their long lost youth and the girls split into giggly groups as if in the school playground.

The only girl not in a group was Jane, the organist, who sat in a corner with Hugh Thomas. I had told him that he need not come since he would not be required for rehearsal. By now, the company were fully aware of the attachment. The announcement of an engagement would come as no surprise to them. It took some time to arrange the men in groups of pirates and to instruct them about their histrionic activities. One group would be playing cards, others drinking from tankards, and Samuel, the Pirate Lieutenant, would be going from one group to another with a flagon, topping up the liquid. There would be laughter and sounds of merriment from the girls as the curtain went up. I had cast Bryn Matthews, a baritone in the Abergelly Male Voice Compliment, as Samuel. For some ten minutes I had tried to show him a 'clumsy' dance he had to perform during the choruses between his solo, which consisted of a step and a hop. This produced ribald remarks from his mates and hysterical laughter from the girls. Bryn was short and fat and totally devoid of any balletic skills, but he had a powerful voice which would raise the rafters in the Welfare Hall.

When order had been restored I reiterated my direction that there was to be a gradual increase of laughter and merriment, reaching a crescendo as the pirates began their opening chorus. What happened was the reverse. Their enthusiasm was overwhelming at the first bar of music. By the fifteenth bar, when they were due to sing 'Pour, oh pour, the pirate sherry', it was exhausted except for a shout of 'Hooray' from Willie James. By the time we had a break for tea, the pirates were beginning to develop into something more than just a male voice choir and were enjoying their new experience. Willie James, in particular, was relishing the opportunity to demonstrate his talent as a ham actor, shouting aloud with what he imagined was a Cornish accent, to the growing annoyance of his fellow pirates. As Gareth Morgan told him during the tea break, 'Willie, it's not the Cornish we recognize in your performance. It's just the corn.'

Eleanor arrived to teach the girls some simple dance steps to follow my rehearsal of their entrance as they come into the cove, which Kate describes as 'a picturesque spot'. They are enthralled by what they see, walking daintily on their toes, apparently stepping over damp places in the sand and discussing shells which attract their attention.

Apart from a few Amazons who made a flat-footed appearance on the scene, the girls gave quite a convincing impression of Victorian young ladies at the seaside. 'Definitely more promising than the Pontywen first rehearsal,' commented my wife. 'We shall have to hide the clodhoppers in the back row of the chorus once again, or perhaps give them exemption from the choreography as a last resort. I see our young Lothario is here, dancing attendance on his beloved. Who would have thought that the dedicated sportsman, to whom rugby and cricket were next to God in his order of priorities, would be spending an evening watching a rehearsal in which he was not involved. I know I professed a match but I did not anticipate such a sudden total surrender. I wonder what his parents think of this development.'

As if on cue, Dr and Mrs Thomas came into the church hall. Eleanor was about to take the floor for the dancing lesson when she recognized the visitors. In the meantime, Hugh was engrossed in a head-to-head conversation with Jane in a corner of the room behind the piano. Eleanor nudged me and whispered, 'Look who's here.' We both advanced on the couple, who were grim-faced. 'How nice to see you,' said my wife.

'We have just come from Hugh's digs,' replied his father. 'His landlady told us he is here at a rehearsal.'

By now everybody in the room was aware of the visit, except the two lovebirds. 'He is there, just behind the piano, talking to Jane,' I said. 'Hugh!' I shouted. 'Your parents are here.' My Curate shot to his feet. His face was ashen.

'We have just had your letter,' were the first words his father spoke when they met. 'Perhaps we can go somewhere and discuss its contents.' There was a silence as the young man sought to come to terms with the situation. 'This is Jane,' he announced.

His father said, 'Hello, Jane.'

His mother said nothing and glared at the embarrassed girl.

'Now then, shall we go back to your digs and have a long talk,' went on Dr Thomas.

Eleanor came to the rescue. 'Jane, will you come and join the rest of the chorus for the dance rehearsal. I hope you don't mind me intruding,' she said, 'but we have to get on with this first step in our preparation.' Hugh's beloved made a speedy escape from her predicament. 'Come on, girls,' ordered my wife, 'let's see you all on the floor and then I'll get you into two lines ready for your ballet.' I had never seen my Curate so deflated. He left the hall with his head bowed, walking between his mother and father as if he were a prisoner being escorted into a prison van.

When we were back at the Vicarage and enjoying a night-cap in the comfort of our armchairs, I said to Eleanor, 'What an eventful evening! We have witnessed the birth of another Gilbert and Sullivan Society and what might be the death of a great romance.'

'I don't know about that,' she replied. 'I agree about the birth but I am not at all sure about the death. Hugh is a very strong character. He will not allow his parents to dictate what is to happen in his love life. If it means that he has to go ahead without the parental blessing, I am positive that he will do so. It will be very interesting to hear from him what has happened when you meet tomorrow morning.'

It was a very worried curate who appeared at Matins

that day. He mumbled his responses and his reading of the lessons. When the service was over he said, 'Would you mind very much if I take my day off today, Vicar? I have a number of things to sort out urgently.'

'By all means, Hugh,' I replied. He was out of the vestry immediately before anything more could be said.

'Well?' my wife asked when I returned to the Vicarage. 'What has happened?' 'What has happened,' I replied, 'is that he requested that he could have his day off today instead of tomorrow. On being told that he could, he was out of the vestry in a flash. He had said that he wanted to sort out a number of things urgently. He looks as if he has all the cares of the world on his shoulders.'

'My dear Fred,' said Eleanor, 'those shoulders are broad enough to carry them, believe me. At least he is a man of action. Those cares will not be there for long. You might even find that when he meets you for Matins tomorrow they will have disappeared.'

'We shall see,' I replied.

She was right. He breezed into the vestry the next morning with a smile on his face. 'Obviously,' I said, 'you have sorted things out.'

'Quite right, Vicar,' he replied. 'I'll tell you about it after the service.' It was a different man, sitting opposite me in the choir stall. He read the prayers in his best Olivier manner, and spent a few minutes on his knees at the end of Matins, apparently in thanksgiving for his deliverance from his problems.

'Come into the Vicarage for a coffee, Hugh,' I suggested, 'and you can let me have a rundown on the events of yesterday in the comfort of our sitting-room.'

We came into the house as Eleanor was on her way out to the surgery. 'Good morning, Dr Secombe,' said my Curate beaming broadly.

'Good morning, Hugh,' replied my wife, 'you look very happy, I must say.' She gave me one of those 'I told you so' looks and went down the steps to her car before he had time to reply.

Once Mrs Cooper had brought in a tray of coffee and biscuits, he proceeded to give me an account of the previous day's happenings. 'As you saw the night before last, my parents came into the hall in high dudgeon to find out if I had taken leave of my senses by getting engaged after such a short acquaintance with Jane. We had a very heated and unpleasant argument at my digs, which ended with them storming out to their car. I am a firm believer in striking when the iron is hot, and I can tell you that it was very hot that night. So I drove to my home yesterday morning. I knew my mother would be on her own and she was the more aggressive. If I could convince her that I had made up my mind to marry Jane come hell or high water, the problem would be solved. My father would fall into line my way.

'She was in the garden collecting a few roses for a vacant vase. I had decided to play my only child role. She had doted on me in my early years. I went to her and put my arms around her. "You needn't try the soft soap approach with me, Hugh," she said. Then to my amazement she told me after they had returned from Abergelly, she and my father had talked long into the night and then decided that, since I was such an obstinate individual, it was pointless trying to change my mind. The one thing they would insist on was that the engagement would be long enough to ensure that Jane and I were in a sound financial position by the time we were married. I stayed for lunch. My father was quite affable. It was obvious that it was he who had persuaded my mother to change her mind. There was just one more obligation to fulfil before making our engagement public. I met Jane as she came out of the office and drove her to her home. She had spent a sleepless night worrying about my parents' hostility. When we arrived at Glamorgan Terrace I asked her father for her hand in marriage. Needless to say he was delighted to give it. Jane had said nothing about the scene in the church hall when she came home. Otherwise it might have been different. So there you are, Vicar. That's it in a nutshell.'

'Hardly a nutshell, Hugh,' I replied. 'It would be a very large nut to contain such a saga. Anyway, thank you for telling me. I am so glad that the air has been cleared. Now you can concentrate your mind on your ordination.'

The days before the ordination sped quickly, and in no time at all I had to concentrate my mind on the sermon I had to preach at the service. Hugh had gone up to the episcopal residence to a retreat conducted by the Bishop for the two days before his entry into the priesthood. I remembered my experience some sixteen years earlier, when the kindly prelate assured his ordinands that there should be no doubt in their minds why they were there in his private chapel. 'God has called you, and from tomorrow you will be his dedicated servants until the end of your lives. Once a priest, always a priest.' There was such a sense of certainty conveyed not only by his words but by his saintly presence that whenever I was plagued by the inevitable challenges in my ministry I had only to recall that quiet moment on the eve of my ordination into holy orders.

By now I had built up an imposing library of theological text books and collections of sermons. I spent all Friday morning reading through all the relevant material. My wife had urged me to write out my sermon. I knew I could not read the complete script from the pulpit lectern, I had to look at my congregation. However, I thought if I made a compromise and had a skeleton of my address, that would be some kind of insurance against a loss of nerve. I wrote out some telling phrases from the theological giants and linked them with the bare bones of my theme. On Friday evening Eleanor and I had sprawled out on the settee in the sitting-room.

'Remember that occasion when you went up into the pulpit at the Mothers' Union service and discovered at the last moment there was no Bible in the lectern?' she said. 'That was a fiasco because there was no text in front of you. Since you are taking the bare minimum of notes with you I trust you have written the text in large letters at the beginning of your learned discourse.'

'My dear Eleanor,' I replied, 'I am positive that there will be a Bible in the cathedral pulpit. In any case, I have written the text at the beginning of my sermon. My headache will not be reading the text but confining my attention to my script. However, I have my theme firmly fixed in my mind and should I by any chance forget to bring my work of art with me, I can tell you now that my text is "I am the good shepherd".'

'In that case,' she said, 'if you arrive in the pulpit without it and stare at the congregation I shall stand up and shout "I am the good shepherd." I can guarantee that the ordinands and the congregation will never forget that text.'

'I suppose that I could always say that the introduction had been carefully rehearsed,' I replied, 'but I do not think that the Bishop would be well pleased. Since you have made such a song and dance about it, I am quite sure that I shall not be left staring open-mouthed at my listeners in the cathedral.'

She gave me a hug and kissed me. 'Just pulling your leg,' she said.

The next morning we joined the forty-seater bus ordered by Tom Beynon from the Western Welsh Company. An enthusiastic contingent of parishioners had gathered outside the church in glorious sunshine to travel to the Cathedral. Hugh Thomas had endeared himself to them in the twelve months he had been in Abergelly. There were ten from Brynfelin, including Janet Rees and her parents, Mrs Roberts and Eddie, and Mr and Mrs Gareth Morgan. Apart from the obnoxious fumes from the churchwarden's ancient pipe, it was a pleasant journey and we arrived in good time.

When I went into the clergy vestry the first person I met was the Dean. He was a venerable figure with a white goatee beard and a reputation for lapses of memory. It was said of him that on one occasion when the choir and the clergy were waiting for him to say the vestry prayer before entering the cathedral, he stood in silence trying to remember the appropriate collect. Then in desperation he said,

'One, two, three, four, five, six, seven – Our father who art in heaven, Amen. Now then, shall we go in?' He opened up the cupboard reserved for the dignitaries. 'Put your jacket in there, Vicar,' he said. Since it was full of robes with no hook available, I wondered where I was supposed to put it. As I stood, jacketless, in my bracered trousers and shirt, and holding the garment at arm's length, the Dean disappeared into the chancel. I decided to deposit the jacket in my case once I had extracted my robes from it.

At that moment, the Bishop entered. 'How good to see you, Fred,' he greeted me with a smile, and then suggested that I put my jacket in the cupboard.

'It seems to be full,' I replied.

'In that case,' said his worship, 'we shall have to make room for you. I'll remove my robes and that will release one hook for you.'

He proceeded to take out his regalia and placed them on the table. I put my jacket on the episcopal hook and unpacked my robes.

While I was doing this, he said, 'I expect you know the procedure prior to your sermon. When the Gospel ends, the verger will come to escort you to the pulpit. After your sermon, once again he will precede you back to your place. Then of course for the laying on of hands you will come into the sanctuary to be one of those who will lay hands on your Curate and the others to be priested.'

A quarter of an hour later I came out of the clergy vestry with the Canon in Residence, the Dean and the Bishop, into the choir vestry where the minor canon, parochial clergy, the cathedral choir and the ordinands were waiting. There was a silence as we looked at the

Dean to lead us in prayer. My irreverent hopes of a repeat of the arithmetical exercise were dashed when the Dean ordered the Reverend Tom Evans, the minor canon, to call on the Almighty. The young man intoned his prayer impeccably in a delightful tenor voice, to which the choir responded with an equally impeccable Amen in full harmony. I tried to attract Hugh's attention before we moved out into the cathedral but his head was kept down.

Once I was in my place in the chancel I tried to see if I could catch sight of Eleanor and my parishioners in the large congregation. The opening hymn was almost over before I spotted them at the back of the church. Hugh's parents were very visible in one of the front pews reserved for relatives of the ordinands. By the time the litany had been sung and the candidates had been examined by the Bishop, my stomach had begun to churn with an attack of nerves. I wished that his worship had never asked me to preach. Then all too soon the verger came to lead me to the pulpit. As I went up the steep steps, hitching up my cassock to avoid an unseemly trip, I dropped the sheet of paper which contained the skeleton of my address. The verger made a neat one-handed catch and came up the steps to hand it to me with a smile on his face.

That smile put me at my ease. I placed the paper on the lectern, announced to the standing congregation that I was preaching in the name of the Father, the Son and the Holy Ghost, and then ignored the script for the whole of the sermon. I spoke of the calling of every priest to be a true shepherd to his flock, to be seen out and about in the parish, since his flock was not limited to his congregation but to all who lived within the parochial boundaries.

I quoted the advice given by a Vicar to a backsliding curate who spent more time in his digs than outside them, claiming that he was improving his spiritual life by reading theology. 'You must wear out the soles of your shoes, my boy, not the seat of your pants.' I emphasized the need for a sense of humour in the priesthood. 'This means that you can laugh at yourself. You will avoid pomposity. It will offset the trials and tribulations which will come upon you. So if you have no sense of humour, develop one. The Good Shepherd had one.' I used references in the Gospels to illustrate it. 'The next time you announce the hymn, "O happy band of pilgrims" look around at the faces of your congregation. If that will not make you want to laugh, nothing will.' It was not an erudite sermon, in any sense of the word, but it did evoke a favourable response from the congregation, who must have been relieved not to hear a doctrinal exposition which was miles above their heads. On a couple of occasions I had a few laughs at the stories I told.

When I went down on my knees back at my place, it was not only to thank God for directing my thoughts but from the sheer relief that my ordeal in the pulpit was over. The rest of the service was a great joy to me, especially the laying of hands on my Curate's head, which symbolized a bond between us which I hoped would be strengthened as the years went by. After the minor canon had intoned the vestry prayer at the end of the service, the Bishop shook my hand. 'Thank you, Fred. That was just what I wanted from you. I am sure these young men must have gained much from your words.'

After I had signed the register, and unrobed, I went into the choir vestry where the newly ordained were gathered.

Hugh came up to me. 'Great, Vicar. What a difference from the treatise inflicted on us a year ago. Would you like to come with me to meet my parents. I am hoping I shall be able to introduce them to Jane's mother and father. If you are with me when that happens, it will be a great help.' We went out together into the throng outside the cathedral.

To our surprise we found both sets of parents were in earnest conversation with Eleanor and Jane at the lych gate. 'The others have gone on to the Beehive café as per last year. I suggest that we make up a sextet at the Mile End Hotel. Congratulations, Hugh,' Eleanor kissed him, then turned and gave me a very warm embrace. 'Darling, you were wonderful,' she whispered in my ear. In the meantime the other four were queuing up to congratulate Hugh.

As we made our way down the street towards the Mile End Hotel, I said to my wife, 'How did you manage to arrange this meeting?'

'Easiest thing in the world,' she replied. 'I said to Mr and Mrs Rees, once we were off the bus, that if they stayed with me and Jane after the service I would take them down to meet Hugh's parents, who would be marooned in the front pew. It was a very tentative occasion initially but by the time we reached the lych gate, the ice had been broken and the conversation began to flow.'

As a consequence, the walk to the hotel involved the two fathers and two mothers chatting to each other, followed by Hugh and Jane holding hands, with Eleanor and me bringing up the rear. 'Tell me, my dear,' I said to her, 'have you thought about changing your profession? You would make a very good candidate for the diplomatic service.'

'Frederick,' she replied, 'you should know me well enough by now to realize I would be a disaster as a diplomat. It's just that I thought this morning I was the only one who could get the two families together. So I did it.'

Later that afternoon, after a convivial lunch during which Hugh's father and Jane's father discovered that they were distant relatives, and Mrs Thomas and Mrs Rees found they were both dedicated members of the Women's Institute, a foundation was laid for a peaceful path to holy matrimony for the Curate and his fiancée. The doctor and his wife came to see us off in our bus, where a place had been reserved for Hugh on the return journey. It was indeed a happy band of pilgrims who came back to Abergelly.

Next morning was Hugh's début as the celebrant at St David's. We had distributed leaflets around Brynfelin, advertising the fact. I took him to church in my Ford as usual. 'Don't forget,' I reminded him, 'this is the last time you will be chauffeured for this service. From next Sunday on you will have to rely on your museum piece to get you there. You are now fully in charge of the daughter church.'

'Have no fear, Vicar,' he said, 'my trusty steed will not let me down, and I can assure you that I will not let you down. I have my sleeves rolled up and I'm ready to organize the house-to-house visiting on the estate. As you told me in your sermon, I shall be wearing out the soles of my shoes.'

When we went into the church I was taken aback by the size of the congregation. With another quarter of an hour before Holy Communion was due to begin, there were about thirty worshippers present. A few of them had come from Abergelly to support the Curate, but the rest of them were from the estate. Some faces I had never seen before. Eddie Roberts met us as we came down the aisle, beaming with delight. 'I've seen to the altar. Everything's ready. Isn't it wonderful!' he enthused. Jane was at the harmonium, sorting out something as a voluntary. Eventually there were forty-five communicants, by far the majority of whom were newcomers to St David's. Dai Elbow was with Gareth Morgan, acting as sidesman.

'Don't tell me you had spread a rumour that my brother was coming,' I said to him.

'God's honour, Vic, nothing of the sort,' he replied indignantly. 'I tell you what, though. When I was taking the leaflets round, I kept telling them "Come and support the best half-back Abergelly has had for years. It's his church now," I told them. "The least you can do is to show 'im you're behind 'im." '

'Well, whatever you have done Dai, it looks as if it has worked. Let's hope the same number will be here next Sunday,' I said.

As I drove back to the Vicarage I congratulated Hugh on the excellent way in which he had taken the service. 'Thank you, too, Vicar, for your address, and its appeal for their continuing support. As you said, it is not the beginning that matters but what happens afterwards. That applies to me as to the congregation. I hope I shall have the grace to persevere.'

The following Friday I went down to the church hall to see the scouts off for their weekend camp at Llanybedw Woods. There was the typical chaos which attended anything Willie James attempted to organize. Tent pegs were missing. One draw sheet could not be found. Cooking utensils were in short supply. Bevan the coal merchant had provided the lorry which had been hosed down for the occasion. By now it had been provided with a new tail-board after the fiasco with the church hall piano. Harry Williams, the driver, was concerned to be off in time in order to get back for his pint at the 'Red Cow'. The younger members of the troop were performing their version of an Indian war dance around the lorry. An hour later, after Willie had gone home to collect the missing items, the yelling mob departed for the journey of fifteen miles to Llanybedw as if they were destined to reach the Australian outback. As usual, Lulu, my faithful hound, had accompanied me in the passenger seat, sitting up like the Duchess she was, completely unamused by the antics of the scouts. According to Eleanor, there were signs she would have to be collected by her breeder for mating with another member of the canine aristocracy.

However, it was not Lulu who sat in the front seat on Sunday morning when I drove to Llanybedw for morning service. My wife had expressed a strong desire to come with me. She had a high opinion of the Reverend Will Evans. It was another sunny day in a sequence of fine weather. Reservoirs were suffering as a consequence. As far as I was concerned, the high pressure could sit over the country for the rest of the summer. I loved the sun and I was enjoying the journey through mountain scenery set against a clear blue sky.

At least it was a clear blue sky until we approached the village of Llanybedw. Billows of black smoke surmounted the forest behind the church. 'Willie James,' we said in one voice. In no time at all we arrived outside the church gates. When we got out of the car we could see flames shooting up, and the noise of crackling was quite fearsome. The Vicar came out to meet us. 'I've phoned the fire brigade,' he told us. 'They are sending out two engines, but I don't think that will be enough. The boys are all safe but apparently the tents and their equipment have been destroyed. Under the circumstances I have decided to cancel the service. When I saw them a few minutes ago they were more concerned about going home than coming to church. Your little scoutmaster is beside himself. It seems he was giving a demonstration of how to light a fire so that the two lads in charge of cooking could get to work while the rest were in church. In a few seconds there was one almighty blaze. So they ran down from the woods as fast as they could.'

'Where are they now, Will?' I asked.

'They are outside the village pub,' he replied. 'The scoutmaster has phoned the lorry owner to come and pick them up.'

When we drove down to the 'White Hart' we discovered a disconsolate, smoke-blackened troop of scouts, silent and sitting on the wall outside the pub car park. A bedraggled Willie James came to meet us. He was like a miner who had just finished his shift. Blinking at us through his spectacles, he said, 'As soon as I put a match to the big pile of brushwood we had gathered, that was it. Everything was on fire at once. I told the boys to get out of the way at once. Nobody is hurt, thank God, but all our camping equipment is gone, and all the blankets and things the lads had brought with them.'

By now the two fire engines were on their way up the hillside. 'I think we had better get back to Abergelly and let everybody know that you are all OK, in case it comes on the Welsh news on the wireless,' I said.

'That's your excuse,' commented Eleanor later. 'It's just a ruse to avoid preaching a sermon and to put your feet up while your Curate is slaving away in the parish church. By the way, whoever commissioned Willie as a scoutmaster? They must have been very short at the time.'

Looking at Willie I remarked, 'It proves they couldn't have been shorter.'

No sooner had we pulled up outside the Vicarage front door than Mrs Cooper came running down the steps in great distress. 'The children opened the back door and Lulu has gone off with that alsatian sheepdog from up the road.'

'There goes our lucrative trade in Cruft-registered boxer puppies,' I said to Eleanor.

As I spoke, the strains of the concluding hymn emerged from the church: 'Through all the changing scenes of life.' 'In trouble and joy,' commented my wife. 'Over the past few months we have had more than our fair share of trouble and precious little joy.'

'Heaviness endureth but a night but joy cometh in the morning,' I replied.

'I don't know what's holding her up,' she replied, 'but we can certainly do with a change of scene.'

we can certainly do with a large dose.